# RETURNING EAST

## LAUCA

# Copyright

©2022 Lauca

Visit the webpage Returning East for an overview of the websites where you can order the book.

First edition

ISBN print:     978-3-9824160-0-7

ISBN digital:   978-3-9824160-0-4

# Chapter 1

In the Joliette harbour, JJ looked down from the deck of the *Cambodge* as a sea of passengers queued to board the ship. Most of the passengers were men. An entire army division was probably heading to Indochina to support the troops in the ongoing battle at Điện Biên Phủ. Priests and nuns were the next conspicuous group, unintentionally mixing with the soldiers on the gangway. Some soldiers gave way and made the sign of the cross; others turned their backs on the ecclesiastical company and kept their distance, thus blocking the priests and the extreme unction that their presence on board seemed to announce.

The mix of passengers included a statesman with his entourage, as well as a few civil servants of lower grade, some in the company of their wives and children. The navy officials completed the picture. With their white uniforms, they looked clean and smart, and they granted a holy quality to the entire scene, as if the passengers were entering the officialdom of marriage. The various groups added brushes of colour to the white background: shades of green for the military, black and white for the missionaries, a pot-pourri of hues for the other passengers. Some glamourous ladies attracted looks, their wasp-like waists eclipsed by their full breasts and large light-coloured hats, whose ivory or vanilla colour often matched that of their purses. Each tone had its own modulation of buzzing voices, which were drowned out by the ship's foghorn.

Jean Jacques stretched his neck in all directions to see if he could glimpse anyone close to his age among the passengers. Seeing no one, he lowered his head to look at the seawater splashing in the gap between the pier and the ship. The size and beauty of the *Cambodge* was remarkable. He read that the ocean liner—162 metres long with a speed of 23 knots—was quite new; its maiden trip had been only the year before. He took in every detail, which he planned on telling George about.

As the ship pulled out of the harbour, he felt the full power of its steam turbine engine, as if he were sitting in a fast car. When the harbour disappeared from sight, he walked to one of the deck chairs and sat down, enjoying the last rays of the afternoon sun. He opened his diary and read again the letter he wrote the night before.

*My dear George,*
*This will be my last letter for a while. I am leaving tomorrow for China. Yes, you heard right, China! I wanted to write to you earlier, but the preparations have taken all my time. I arrived in Marseille today, and I will board a ship of the Messageries Maritimes, which will take me to Shanghai.*

*I know what you are thinking. I also feel I must apologise for changing my mind about going to Asia again. Despite my mixed feelings, I need to go there. I have good reasons and I hope you will understand my position.*

*My neighbour, my teacher, Old Min, passed away a few weeks ago. He found out he was very sick just a while before. After several years of searching, he had finally located his long-lost daughter and had recently got in touch with her. He was, though, too sick to go back to China to see her and she has no means to come to France. It was a sad moment for him to realise that, you can imagine.*

*Old Min was a generous and wonderful teacher, who dreamt of spreading the traditions of Chinese painting in France and preserving this ancient art. Unfortunately, his poor health prevented him from seeing his dream realised. I see now that he probably sensed he had not much time left to live. This is why Old Min took me in as his student, with an unspoken wish that I would carry on his work. He treated me with such kindness and selflessness; he guided me and took his time to teach me. During his stay at the hospital, we discussed the possibility of my going to China to study painting there. Old Min even contacted one of his friends, who is the dean of an academy in Hangzhou. Of course, I did not want to go. But I could not tell Old Min that, as he lay on his deathbed. Instead, I humoured him and promised that I would go. What a mistake!*

*On one of my last visits, he asked me to take his ashes to his daughter, so that he could rest in peace in his motherland. Despite the pain, which made his face contract and his hands tremble, he took my hand and pressed in it a ticket to China and a letter from his friend in Hangzhou, who had accepted me as a student for the next few months! You can imagine my surprise, and my fear. I was dumbfounded, and I just took the ticket. The day after, though, after a sleepless night, I planned to tell him I could not go. When I arrived at the hospital, his bed was empty. I had arrived too late. What would you have done in my position, George, tell me? How can I now refuse to go, without having told him so? His wish to let his daughter have his ashes mattered to him so much that he arranged my ticket from his hospital bed! I feel I cannot let him down now. The dean's letter allowed me to secure a visa to China, but I am not sure I will go to the academy. Still, I must meet Old Min's daughter and give her his ashes.*

*You see, I have very good reason to go there. And this time I want to keep my promise.*

*I shall write to you more from the ship, maybe send you postcards along the way, if possible. I don't know. Old Min bought a third-class ticket, but my parents changed it to a tourist-class ticket, not the cheapest. At the beginning, I thought my father would not let me travel. But it looks like they are keen to see me go, after all. Especially my mother, I am sure. Maybe my father agreed in the hope that the experience will forge my character. You know him too. He has clear ideas how a man must behave in society, and shyness is not allowed.*

*Since Old Min passed away, I did not have anybody to speak to. We did not speak a lot either, but I felt he was my close friend. Now I feel lonelier than ever, and you, George, are my only friend.*

*My warmest regards to you. JJ.*

JJ closed his diary and, as usual, he tried to recall George's baby face. When the memory failed to bring George's face with precision, he looked at the portrait in his diary. Each time he bought a new diary, he would draw George's portrait again: a child of six or seven in blue shorts and a white shirt, a leather ball in his hand, his eyes half closed and facing the sun but still looking straight into the camera. The image was like a picture he had stolen from his mother shortly after George's funeral.

***

As the first gleam of neon lighting appeared on deck, he sat up and realised he had dozed off. He hurried back to his cabin, where he had left his belongings. He found the cabin bare, with only four bunk beds and spare furniture; on each bed was a set of luggage, its owner probably still on deck. He looked for his bags and took the largest one next to him. He dipped one hand inside, searching until something soft brushed his fingers: he knew it was the white silk scarf carefully wrapped around a little blue urn. He had admired this small ceramic urn and its intricate pattern of white clouds thousands of times at Old Min's, but at that time, he could not have imagined what its purpose would be. He took the bundle out and unwrapped the scarf to check that the urn's lid was still secure; it had looked slightly loose on one side when the employee of the funeral home gave him the urn, and he had wrapped it with hemp thread to keep the lid in place.

JJ's bed was on an upper berth next to the porthole, which he opened now to look out. His heart gave a little jump at the smell of the sea, a familiar feeling suddenly rushing in. True, he had taken this route twice already in his life, but somehow, he had kept no concrete memories. In those four or five years he had spent abroad, he lived withdrawn in his drawings, almost never leaving the family residence. He wondered how it was possible that he could still remember such a smell, like a fresh sea scent mixed with the stench of gasoline that was strongest when they left a harbour. He recalled the smells of food on those voyages and noted that there were none this time; the cabin was probably farther away from the kitchen. He was taking a deep breath in when the cabin's door swung open. A man of his age greeted JJ with a vibrant and warm voice, introducing himself as Frédéric Maréchal.

'Our family name is marshal but we never had anything to do with the army. No idea where the name came from,' Frédéric said, shaking his head at the unasked question. 'We are, rather, a merchant family, always have been. But my old folks had always been in the small game. Two or three shops tops, nothing exciting. Since the illness of our father, my brother took over and we got into the big business. We're new money, very, very new!' He laughed and his eyes brightened, the corners of his mouth reaching his ears.

JJ gave him a short-lived smile while he took in Frédéric's size. He was in black trousers and a cream jacket, whose lapels were partially covered by the collar of his white shirt. Frédéric sat on the lower berth next to JJ and crossed his legs, leaning his torso towards JJ.

'I'm here with my brother. We are with the trade delegation heading to Shanghai. A minor politician, a Mr Dupont, is the head of the delegation. Have you seen him? A real colony man, pompous and self-content like those in the gossip magazines. Not that I am reading those,' he said, retreating his body a little, 'my mother does. I'm glad my brother took the tourist class, so that we can keep some distance. Join us for dinner! We are going to spend the next month together in any case, so we better become friends and have a jolly time together. How old are you, chap?'

JJ took a moment to realise Frédéric had asked him a question. 'Twenty-three in one month.'

'In one month? We'll be in China by then. Jolly, you'll have a different birthday this year! I am twenty-five and a half, he added and puffed his chest out. He decided to take his jacket off seconds later.

'Say, have you seen the troops? What do you think, my friend? Are we going to lose Indochina? My brother says so and that's why he wants to make new contacts in China. No more rubber. Let's import silk! Brilliant plan, don't you think?'

The flood of words drowned the memories, which threatened to resurface in JJ's mind. He tried but failed to recall the last time someone his age had talked to him so with such enthusiasm. He took a long, unseen breath to keep himself from crying.

'What is it? Do you feel unwell? I have medicine, if you feel sick', Frédéric said, opening his luggage to take out another jacket in a lighter colour.

'No, no, it is just the sea air that makes my eyes water,' JJ replied, getting up to close the porthole and his pain.

'I see. Frédéric changed his classic jacket for a more fashionable one; he looked at his reflection in the half-body mirror hanging on a wall, a little smile on his face. 'Let's go to the dining hall. They will serve soon dinner, pal. Your name is Jean Jacques, you said?'

'Yes,' JJ said, and after some hesitation, he added, 'actually many call me JJ.'

'JJ! This is much better. I'll call you JJ too. You can call me Fred. We are going to share the cabin for an entire month. We can be friends.'

And with these few words, Fred replaced JJ's world with his own.

# Chapter 2

After a few ups and downs along the stairs and wrong turns, JJ and Fred reached the dining hall. Large windows graced the lengths of the two sides of the hall; on sunny days, the light flowing in only enhanced the gold of the lilium flowers decorating the thick blue carpet. Above the passengers, lilium leaves and stems were painted on the wooden box ceiling, creating a white and green forest hovering overhead. Four or six cream-coloured dining chairs with blue cushions surrounded tables with beige tablecloths. Crystal glasses, silver cutlery, and rich blue napkins glowed under warm table lamps. The golden mirrors at the back of the hall reflected the countless lamps, giving the hall an extra glimmer. Often the captain proudly mentioned the article published in a design magazine about the opulence and elegance of the *Cambodge*'s dining hall.

'Wow, this is spectacular,' Fred said. 'This is a real luxury. Look at the lamps and all those mirrors.'

A waiter greeted them with a polite smile. 'May I have your cabin number, sirs?'

'Twenty-four,' Fred replied.

One of the waiter's eyebrows raised half a centimetre. 'Twenty-four? Your dining hall is on the deck below. You can take the stairs on your left; the entrance is just a few steps down the corridor.'

'What's the difference? I like this dining hall better. Why can't we stay here?'

'I am afraid it is not possible, sir. All tables are reserved.'

'No, they are not. There are several which are still free. Shouldn't it be first come, first served?'

JJ shifted his weight from one foot to the other. 'Fred, let's go. This is for the first class.'

'So what? Are we not worthy of first class, or what? Is it money? I can pay you extra to dine here.' And he plunged his right hand into his trouser pocket.

JJ clutched his arm. 'Let's go, Fred. The dining room of the tourist class is nice. I saw some pictures.'

'Indeed, sir,' the waiter said with a grateful look at JJ. 'We pride ourselves on offering only the best in each class. I am sure the food won't disappoint you either.'

Fred's face was still pouting, but he followed JJ down the stairs, giving the waiter one last hard stare.


As soon as they reached the lower deck, Fred's mood lifted.

'I knew of course it was not our dining hall. But let me tell you this, JJ,' he said with a large smile, 'money can do wonders and… ' His smile died when they entered their dining hall.

JJ seemed stunned, too. 'Well, I guess the photos only showed the best angles.'

They looked at the long, laminate green tables with brown plastic chairs. A hanging lamp attached to the white ceiling illuminated every other table by a loop of black plastic cord.

'This is awful,' Fred said, appalled. 'He said the best in each class? Did he mean the class for pig farmers? The tables don't even have tablecloths.'

'I agree that it is not as lavish, but look, those wooden panels are quite nice,' JJ said, pointing to one side of the hall.

'This looks like the canteen of my old school. It's all cheap plastic. Even the green reminds me of my school.'

'Yes, they could have chosen better colours to go with the wooden panels. But apparently the Formica tables are very fashionable nowadays.'

'And is the smell also fashionable?' Fred said, turning up his nose.

JJ caught a whiff of bleach and fried oil. 'Maybe they have just cleaned the hall,' he said, looking for signs of a recent scrubbing.

With a worried look, JJ watched his new acquaintance walk towards a waiter, ready to complain. A voice from the back of the room stopped him.

'Ah, there is my brother, Marcel, still with the two Englishmen,' Fred said, turning to JJ. 'We met them as we boarded. One is an English lawyer, he's staying in our cabin, the other a bank clerk. Let's go join them.'

Fred and JJ approached the group while conversations floated around the room. The men embarked on arduous introductions, French and English words sparring with each other and getting mixed up.

His mouth partially open, Fred listened to the unfamiliar sounds coming out of his brother's mouth. He turned to JJ with bright eyes. 'My brother learnt English with the resistance. He fought alongside the English.'

JJ wondered whether Marcel was much older than Fred, or whether he looked so old because of the war. Tall, with a sturdy figure like his younger brother, he appeared manly and poised. His bass voice even reminded JJ of his own father. But unlike JJ's father, Marcel looked poised without being authoritative. Marcel's similarities with his father and the mix of languages brought forth in JJ memories of dinner parties that his parents organised during the war. French was mostly spoken, but English was too when they had foreign guests or Japanese officials coming by. JJ could speak some too, thanks to his mother. English lessons were one of the rare moments when he could spend time with his mother during their years abroad.

JJ did not join the conversation. He followed along, his head halfway bent, his eyes now on Fred and now on the other passengers, not giving away how much he could understand. He used to do that a lot, especially in Indochina, where his dislike for the country, for its distance from France, made him mute and aloof as a form of resistance to a life he did not want.

'JJ, how come you are going to China?' asked Marcel, swinging the conversation back to French.

'I study fine arts,' JJ replied, not wishing to talk about Old Min.

'Arts in China? Really? I was not aware they had any. In Shanghai? Where will you stay?' Marcel asked, filling his mouth with a large bite of pepper entrecote.

'I have a letter of recommendation for the Central Academy of Fine Arts in Hangzhou. My teacher was a former schoolmate of the dean.'

'Ah, I see. Good, good. It will do you good to see the world a bit. Will make you a man. This is what I always tell my little brother. Travel, start a business'—his head slightly sinking forward, his gaze intense, 'get to know the local beauties.' He burst out in a laugh that shook his head back and forth. Fred joined him, while JJ gave a brief smile.

A rush flowed through JJ's body again, his mind pushing fragments of old conversations back to the unconscious mind. He glanced at Fred and at the guests in the dining hall, heard the clink of cutlery and glasses accompanying laughter, and then he looked at Marcel again.

JJ spent the remainder of the dinner half in a trance, swallowing the rest of the meat on automatic pilot and pushing his canned green beans from one side of the plate to the other. As soon as his table companions finished their food, he excused himself and disappeared, returning to the cabin only after everybody was asleep.

The following day he woke up before the others; he picked up a nondescript grey folder bound with an elastic band and set off for breakfast. The dining hall was quite empty, and he let his eyes wander around the room undisturbed. The passengers were well-dressed as they were the evening before, but he knew that at some point on the trip, the self-imposed decency would fade. Especially for the ladies. They would show up with their hair untied because the seasickness would give them a little rest, just like his mother; or they would get fun-loving and flirtatious, again, just like his mother had.

After breakfast, he walked up and down the ship to explore the different areas; there were two hairdressers, a smoking room, a reading room. He also discovered the ironing room and the laundry room. He remembered that on his first voyage, he had hidden himself in the laundry room. It was where only a few people bothered to go, least of all his parents, the rare times they were looking for him.

The weather was fine; still, the lack of sun meant a thick jacket was needed to stay outside. JJ found a spot on the deck that offered shelter from the occasional gust of wind and sat with a content smile. He opened his folder and took out first his sketch pad, then the coloured pencils, the eraser, and the watercolours. He sighed after he realised he did not have any water with him. *Oh well, the coloured pencils will do for now.* He picked up a pencil as blue as the sky above him and immersed himself in drawing.

At dinner time, he joined the others in the dining hall.

'JJ, where have you been? I did not see you the whole day,' Fred said when JJ joined him at the table, where Marcel and the two Englishmen were again deep in conversation. 'You missed the Tunisian coast. The boat sailed so close that with binoculars, you could see real Bedouins.'

'He was probably trying to get rid of you, chatty old lady,' Marcel said. 'JJ is obviously a quiet and well-behaved man, who does not jump like a puppy at the sight of something new.' He extended one hand to hit his brother in the head and added, 'And the Bedouins live in the desert, you ignorant little brat.'

Fred's face flushed as he kept a hand on the spot where Marcel had hit him and said nothing for a while. He waited for the conversation among the Englishmen and his brother to continue before directing his attention to JJ again.

'Maybe they were not Bedouins, but they had camels. They had turbans on their heads and looked old and sunburnt.'

JJ let Fred tell him all about what he saw and did during the day, again with a touch of envy for the energy his new friend displayed.

'Your turn now,' Fred said when he had stopped talking.

'What?'

'Yes, tell me how you spent your day. What did you do? I know you did not sleep, at least not in the cabin, as I went back there several times to see if you were there.'

JJ hesitated. His father's voice came to him. They were in the studio, his father sitting in the dark brown leather armchair, the atmosphere here so different from the light and cool living room with white rattan furniture.

'JJ, a man must know how to make polite conversation about everything, even if he knows nothing.'

JJ once asked his mother how he could do that.

'Talk about the weather, food, or the latest book, if you want to be taken for an intellectual,' she had replied. 'And if you lack topics, tell the ladies how charming they look and the men how smart they are.'

JJ turned to Fred and started talking in a moderate pitch. 'I woke up early and had breakfast. I think the cook is doing a good job with the food. The croissants were not unlike those one could get back home. I then stayed on one of the decks to read a little, and I do believe I fell asleep there.'

'That's all? You read, you slept, and you ate? My… and I thought before leaving that I had a boring life… ' Fred laughed. 'You didn't see any of the scenery outside. Are you not even a bit excited about the trip?'

JJ thought for a moment. 'I guess I will be excited when I get to China.'

Fred glanced at him between bites and shook his head a little. 'Indeed, you are a quiet one… even your voice is quiet, as if you were in a funeral Mass. A church voice. Do you have brothers or sisters?'

'No, I don't. Only had one cousin,' replied JJ, biting his lips shortly after.

Fred was concentrating on his pêche Melba, which the pretty waitress had just served, and he did not see JJ's gesture. 'A band is playing later on. Let's go listen to it,' he suggested.

JJ shook his hand lightly, stood up, and excused himself as he had the previous evening. Before he left the table, Fred stopped him.

'Ah, I forgot! There is a letter for you,' Fred said, and he took out a crumpled envelope.

'What, a letter? How come?' JJ asked.

'I don't know. A naval officer brought it this morning as we were getting ready for breakfast. I wanted to give it to you earlier, but you were not there.'

JJ took the plain envelope with no other writing but his name. 'It must be from my father. Nobody else would write me here.' He put the letter in his trouser pocket and left the hall.


Back in the cabin, JJ grabbed his grey folder again and went to the lower deck, which he discovered offered a good view and some privacy.

He found the right spot and resumed drawing, working on a sketch of the boarding passengers. The scene was still impressed in his mind, though his hand was drawing more slowly than he wished. Once an art teacher had said that taking too long on a drawing was a sign of a lack of talent, so since then he had tried to linger less on details.

*But Old Min never said anything like that. He encouraged me to paint slowly. He said I could become an excellent painter.*

After half an hour, the paper had turned grey, old lines covered by new ones, which in turn were being erased and redrawn to bring out yet another detail of the scene. JJ looked at his sketch and frowned. He started again, adjusting the size of the silhouettes, his eyes focused on the drawing. Lost in the task, he did not hear the heavy footsteps approaching him.

# Chapter 3

Fred was standing a few steps away from him. 'Here you are. You like hiding… I looked for you everywhere,' he said. 'And you like drawing.' He sat on the chair next to JJ, grabbed a pencil, and scrutinised it.

'Can you give me a piece of paper?' Before JJ could react, he took one.

JJ saw him folding the paper from the right, and the left, then again and again. Fred then took the pencil closest to him and drew a few lines on the folded sheet.

'Here it is! The *Cambodge* in all its majesty.' And he held up a paper boat on which he had drawn two faces looking out of a porthole. 'And here we are, sailing to new adventures, new frontiers and riches.'

JJ looked at him, taken aback, remembering that the last time he had done origami was in Indochina.

Indifferent to JJ's perplexed expression, Fred continued to make up a story of two young heroes fighting adversities, bad weather, and seasickness to reach their destination and get rich.

'Is it you and your brother on the boat?' JJ asked, half giving in to Fred's game.

'My brother? Nooo, he will spend all his time with the Englishmen, or some other member of the delegation, and he already has had plenty of adventures anyway. But there is still space on the boat. Would you like to jump in? You can be my other brother.'

'Brother?' JJ asked in a pitch higher than normal.

'Sure, why not? I told you we can be friends. Maybe after this trip we will become sworn brothers! Who knows what the mysterious Far East has in store for us!'

'I've never had a sworn brother,' JJ said, then lowering his chin and gaze a little, he added, 'I haven't had a friend in a long time.'

Fred slapped his leg with his right hand while he kept the boat in the air with the left. 'No wonder, chap, if you keep hiding. But we can have fun together.'

'I am afraid I am not much fun. And probably not a good friend either.'

'What a pile of rubbish! You are fine, and together we can make an invincible team.' And he stretched his open hand towards JJ.

JJ looked at the hand, unsure what to do. Old Min was his friend. And George before him. What if the past was the same as the future?

Friendships die. Friends die.

Or not?

He stretched his hand out but stopped in mid-air; he then rubbed his palm on his trousers with a slightly flushed face before he finally took Fred's hand and shook it with vigour.

'You and me, friends. I agree,' JJ said in his church whisper.

'Marvellous, JJ,' Fred said. 'But now no more hiding, yes?'

'Right, no more hiding,' he replied. 'Well, unless I need to.' And he laughed so widely he showed his upper gums.

'I know now why you don't laugh much… you want to avoid showing so much of your mouth,' Fred teased.

JJ sealed his lips but kept laughing, basking in the warmth he felt at Fred's joke.

'Did you read the letter? What did your father say?' Fred asked, stretching himself along the deck chair, his hands behind his head and ankles crossed.

'Oh, I completely forgot. I don't think it is anything important though.' JJ took the letter out of his pocket, tore the envelope, and read the thin sheet of paper.

Fred looked at the sky while JJ read. When the silence felt prolonged, Fred turned and even in the dim light, he could see that his friend's face was pale white. The letter in his hand was quivering.

'JJ, what is it? Bad news? Did someone die?' Fred sat up and faced JJ.

His friend stared back with large eyes, and without a word, he got up and left.

'Hey, what is it? You left all your things here… ' Fred shouted after him. *Weird guy*, Fred thought, *but I hope nobody has died. If he disembarks at the next harbour, I will be left alone with my brother. It will be a long, boring trip, almost as bad as travelling with maman.*

Fred collected JJ's art supplies and returned to the cabin, wondering what news had so shaken up his friend.

JJ found the laundry room again and closed the door behind him. Luckily, it was empty. A sudden heaviness obliged him to sit on the tiled floor. The warmth of the room did not stop JJ from shivering as he read the letter again.

Dear JJ,

If you receive this letter, it means that you are on your way to find my daughter and give her my ashes, and it means I can rely on you. I am so thankful for what you are doing; it means a lot to me. My heart is at peace knowing that I will rest in my motherland.

You are a good student and a good person. This is why I ask you here for your help.

My daughter is in a troublesome situation, and she has already had such a hard life, losing her mother many years ago, and me being so far away with no contact. I must make it up to her for being such a terrible father.

My ex-classmate in Hangzhou has a valuable scroll from Qi Baishi, a painter I met when he did some carpenter work at our house. Qi Baishi is now quite famous, and his scroll has become precious. The political situation in China does not allow my friend to sell the scroll. He must even hide the painting as having valuable possessions is not looked upon favourably.

Once you are in Hangzhou, my friend will give you the scroll. I want you to sell it in France, or maybe Hong Kong. The proceeds of the sale must go to my daughter.

I have to warn you that this is not a simple task. Nobody has to know that you have such a scroll, as it is prohibited to export such a piece. But being a student in the academy will give you a reason to carry a scroll with you, and you can hide the Qi Baishi work between two worthless paintings. My daughter needs the money, but nobody should find out where it comes from. The best solution is to use my friend as an intermediary.

I know this is not a simple mission and there might be some risks. I apologise for the trouble. If I am asking you, it is because I have no other way to help my daughter. I caused her so much pain, this is the last thing I can do for her.

I am in your hands; I trust you will fulfil the wishes of your teacher.

Min Bingwen

JJ held the letter up to his eyes to inspect it. He wondered if the letter was really from Old Min. His French was not so good, but the letter had no grammar mistakes in it, nor did it look like Old Min's handwriting. In fact, the writing looked too firm and precise to JJ for it to be done when Old Min was already weak and in the hospital.

JJ lowered the letter. Now he understood why Old Min was so keen for him to go to that Hangzhou academy. But selling a piece of art? He did not know how to do that, and it was illegal. How could he do something like that? His head spun, the last sentence of his teacher's letter burning in his heart.

***

When Fred entered the smoking room, he found his brother still talking to the same Englishmen while they smoked cigars. Fred tried to approach undetected, but Marcel noticed his presence when he was still a few steps away. Earlier, Marcel had told Fred he would tolerate his presence in the smoking room, but he forbade Fred to smoke.

'Ah, tu es là? Why are you not with your friend?' Marcel asked with a serious face.

'He is busy with a letter,' Fred replied in an uncertain voice.

'Well, wasn't there some singing in the music room downstairs? Go and check it out. We are speaking in English here, and you would get bored,' Marcel said. He took a slow pull on his cigar, its end burning into a long and compact cylinder of ash, while Fred watched as if in a trance. Then Marcel turned his back and resumed his conversation, making Fred feel like an unwanted child once again.

Dragging his feet, Fred left the smoking room and made his way downstairs before bumping into JJ.

'My friend, here you are! Didn't we just agree to no more hiding?'

JJ blushed. 'I am sorry. I apologise.'

'Well, no matter, my friend. I hope nothing bad has happened, has it? You are not going to leave us, are you?' Fred furrowed his eyebrows.

JJ shook his head. 'No, no, nothing serious. I was just surprised.'

'Well, then, let's go enjoy some music. You will not leave me alone anymore this evening. We have to celebrate our friendship after all,' Fred said, taking JJ under his arm to pull him along.

The interior of the music room was similar to that of the first-class dining hall, with small tables and lampshades. A quartet of male singers was performing tunes from the twenties.

'Such old music. Why don't they play something more modern?' Fred said.

JJ nodded slightly.

Fred took a gulp of his beer. 'Ah, my brother does not allow me to smoke but at least I can drink.' He put his glass down and bent towards JJ. 'Do you like jazz music? Apparently, they are going to have a jazz festival somewhere in America. Isn't that cool music? I hope they will play some during the journey.'

'I am not very much into music, if at all,' JJ said, turning his full glass in his two hands. 'I sometimes listen to classical music.'

Fred felt deflated at the lack of reaction from JJ. This was his first trip abroad, his debut in the world, and he wanted to have fun. He tried another approach. 'I left your stuff on your bed.'

'Oh, right, I forgot. Thank you, Fred.'

'Say, your drawings are very good. So, you are going to China to study art?'

JJ held his breath and froze for a moment, and Fred waited for a response before he became annoyed at his friend's reluctance to speak.

'I am not sure why I am going there anymore,' JJ finally said.

'You are not sure? See the world, my friend, I told you! The Far East awaits us, Shanghai awaits us! Imagine, maybe something will happen even here, on the ship. Someone could get murdered, and we could help to find the culprit. That would be exciting, don't you think?' Fred asked JJ.

A shiver ran down JJ's spine. 'No, I don't think I would want to be involved in a murder case.'

'Okay, maybe it is too extreme. But what about… a theft! That could be exciting. Who could do it?' Fred looked around the room. 'Look at the couple over there.' He raised his chin to show a round table a few metres away from theirs. A distinguished man with a black moustache and a woman in an evening dress with a plissé skirt were sipping yellow cocktails in long glasses, each topped with an orange slice.

'They don't look like thieves to me. The lady's necklace is probably worth enough to pay for a few trips back and forth in a first-class cabin,' JJ said.

'Yes, but maybe she is the one with the money, and he has nothing. He must find some to make her happy. We should watch out; do you have any valuables with you?'

'Yes… no!' JJ said.

'Yes or no?' Fred asked.

'No, no, it's nothing of real value.'

'What do you mean? Do you have something which looks valuable?'

'Not really. It is just a small ceramic jar. It is a delicate piece, but not worth much money.'

'How do you know?' Fred insisted. He watched JJ think. 'Maybe it is valuable, and you don't know. Better hide it well.'

'I am sure that it is not expensive. My teacher gave it to me. He was not rich. I stored it safely in my luggage.'

'Right, we also have a pack of money with us. My brother did not tell me, but I saw how he took care of hiding it in… ' He stopped, lowering his glass. 'Better not tell you,' Fred said and laughed.

Fred excused himself to go to the men's room and, on his way, he thought about his friend and how he would like very much to see this mysterious ceramic jar.

# Chapter 4

The days passed quickly, and despite the skirmishes between Egyptian and British troops a few years earlier, the passage through the Suez Canal was uneventful.

Lying in his berth, JJ took his diary and glued a postcard of Port Said that Fred had bought for him. He found the card uninspiring. The modern building in the panorama clashed with the image of a black man in traditional clothing; the women in long black veils with two children made him think of poor Madonnas instead of invoking anything exotic. He started writing.

*Dear George,*

*Many greetings from Port Said! Actually, we left it a few days ago already. We are by now close to Djibouti and Somaliland. I apologise for not writing sooner. I expected to have time and serenity during the trip to write to you regularly, but something happened.*

*I share my cabin with two Frenchmen and one Englishman. One of the Frenchmen is around my age and we became friends! We are spending almost all our time together. I don't even get as much time to draw as I wanted. He is a lively person and seldom stops talking. Each time the ship approaches a new harbour for a stopover, Fred (that's his name) is on the deck, ready to get the first glimpse of the wharf. Sometimes he even gets up in the middle of the night to catch the harbour lights. I often accompany him, but I never follow him when passengers can leave the ship for an excursion. I have then a few hours to myself and can draw. He brings me postcards to send. I enjoy his company. He's so energetic and we laugh a lot together. It makes me forget so many things— my mother, Indochina.*

JJ hesitated and then struck out the last sentence. He held his pen, thinking about what to write next, but his brain refused to bring forth any thoughts about the present. Instead, George came to his mind. JJ flipped the pages of his diary to look at the boy's portrait.

His mother once told JJ that he had met his cousin George in France when they were toddlers, but he had no memories of him. He met his cousin again a few days after the family had settled into their new residence in Phnom Penh. JJ and his parents were at his aunt and uncle's house for dinner, and there was George, with his tuft of curly black hair, his bright blue eyes so similar to his father's and uncle's. JJ felt shy and still upset about the long journey by sea, but George just stretched out his hand to pull JJ into his room. His cousin was a chatty little boy, a couple of years younger than JJ, who had just started primary school. George loved nature, and he showed JJ his collection of butterflies and insects. While the insects repelled JJ, he admired the beauty of the butterflies.

'I want to make a list of all the butterflies. My father said for that I need to draw the butterflies.' George took out coloured pencils and made awkward attempts to reproduce one of the butterflies on paper.

JJ looked at them and said, 'If you want, I can help you with the drawing.'

'Really? Can you draw? That would be fantastic,' George said, and he immediately gave JJ the paper and pencils to reproduce the black and yellow butterfly he used as a model.

They spent their first time together quietly, George telling him about his life, and JJ drawing in silence. Since that day, they had a common project: George would catch the butterflies and JJ would draw them. But George loved to spend time outside and he was impatient with the slow progress of JJ's drawing; with the passing of time, George would bring the models to JJ and run off again to catch more butterflies or to explore the surroundings.

The slam of the cabin door brought JJ back to the present. Fred was there, demanding his attention. 'JJ, come, we are approaching Somaliland.' He grabbed JJ's diary from his hand. 'Come on, you can keep writing later.'

By then JJ knew that Fred would not give him peace until JJ gave in, thus he put his diary away and jumped down from his berth.

'I'm ready.'

As the ship entered the gulf of Tadjoura, the two friends saw from the deck steep ridges and continuous plains. Far inland, mountain peaks towered over the landscape. Cranes and unfinished buildings punctuated the French harbour; from a distance, the people looked like ants moving around without aim.

'I want to go back to the cabin,' said JJ, holding his shirt with two hands to keep it from touching his body. They had not been out long, but their shirts were already wet with sweat.

'Come on, you can cool down in front of the cabin ventilator later.'

'I can barely breathe. I'm going back inside.'

33

'No, no, stay. A man has to learn how to suffer,' Fred said in earnest.

'That's what your brother says, I suppose.'

'Yes, yes. He is right. I heard China is very humid, better we get used to it.'

Fred moved to place his arm around JJ's shoulder to keep him from leaving, but as soon as their bodies made contact, Fred recoiled with a disgusted expression on his face. He wiped his wet hand on his trousers.

'Why do you think I want to go inside?' JJ said.

They both laughed.

'Say, you held your ground with my brother well today, talking about that movie,' Fred said. 'I always feel a little intimidated by him, and annoyed. He still treats me like a child, so often I get confused when I speak to him. You, on the other hand, just laid out your cards. I would have never expected that. Chapeau.'

'Oh, I guess it is because I enjoyed the movie. I thought *Holiday for Henrietta* was great. I still cannot understand why he did not like it,' said JJ.

'Maybe, but you were also very chatty with that gentleman from Bretagne when I smoked a cigarette with him.'

'Chatty? It was only small talk while I was on sentry duty to make sure your brother would not see you smoking.'

'Still… you rarely speak with strangers.'

'I hate small talk. I guess that's why I don't have friends. But my father always considered the art of small talk a necessary social skill and he kept me prisoner for hours in his studio, commanding me to practise small talk with him.'

'C'est pas vrai! Did your mother have to practise too?' Fred asked.

'No. She was already proficient at that,' JJ replied and shrugged.

'What's wrong? You don't like your mother?' Fred asked, noticing a dark cloud moving over JJ's face.

'She will not be my mother anymore.' He lowered his voice. 'I am sure she will divorce my father while I am in China.'

Fred clicked his tongue. 'Oh, I guess nowadays it is not that unusual. You still have your father, don't you?'

'I think it won't change much for me. My mother has always been too busy with her life to take care of me, while my father still travels a lot for work.'

'You lucky guy,' Fred said, punching JJ on his upper arm. 'My mother had me when she was older in age so she can't help but supervise me, my health, my friends, like a general inspecting his troops, which of course suits our name.' He laughed. 'I am so glad I finally escaped. I am thankful my brother agreed to take me with him.'

JJ stayed silent for a moment. 'You are the lucky one. I wished my mother would have taken an interest in me and my life.' He paused, as if he forgot something. 'But no chance of that,' he said, shaking his head.

'Come on, it cannot be. The trip costs a fortune even in the tourist class, and if your parents agreed to pay, they must have done so to make you happy. It's how they show you love,' Fred said.

JJ furrowed his brow. 'Money is not really an issue. She is just too selfish to care.'

'Well, if you think so. Forget about her. Now you have me, my brother,' Fred replied, clasping his hand in JJ's as if to seal their friendship.

They turned again towards the approaching harbour and watched as the people got bigger and darker.

'Does your mother prepare your breakfast?' JJ asked Fred.

'Yes, of course. Sometimes she buys fresh croissants; sometimes she bakes.'

'Nice.'

'Yours?'

'Not since I remember.'

'Really? You had to prepare breakfast by yourself as a child?' Fred asked with a surprised look.

'Of course not, we had a nanny.'

'Oh, I never had one.'

'I had many.'

Fred put his foot on the lower bar of the banister and turned towards JJ. 'Sounds like you're going to China to escape your family, too.' He pointed to JJ and added, 'But I tell you, my friend, you've been missing all the fun, hiding on the ship instead of going down with me to explore new lands.'

JJ sneered. 'What an idea! I told you, I am not known to look for fun or be fun myself.'

'But aren't you curious about the other countries? There is a whole new life there. It's exciting!'

'I don't care about it. I am happy to stay on board and draw. I want to become a fine painter.'

JJ returned to the cabin, leaving Fred on the ship deck. He climbed up to his berth and set his diary aside to lie down to think. He wondered how his life would have been if he had a mother like Fred's. He could not imagine his mother in the kitchen baking for him. Not that she would not go in the kitchen at all. When she did, she was mostly busy mixing a cocktail or drinking a glass of wine. Otherwise, she would rather buy already-made food than to cook.

In the past, she had tried to cook during that horrible period when JJ's father would not come home for dinner a few times a week. He was left alone with his mother, who would spend the meal smoking and drinking. He did not know why his father was not there. Certainly, the meals were not as appetising as those they used to have during the war, but they were not that bad. But on those evenings his father was absent, JJ would wish dinner would end as soon as possible. He gulped down his food, something his father would not have allowed, yet his mother never reproached him for. This lasted several years, until one day his mother disappeared. JJ thought she had left for good. One morning, he got up and a nanny was there, informing him that his mother was away for a while. He could still feel how the blood had left his body. He was sure she would never come back again. The simple recollection of that day made his chest tight… she had not even bothered to say goodbye to him.

But one day she did come back. She was there again, physically at least. She still did not look after him, but she was home. At that time, he was glad she had returned, but now he realised it had been pointless. Looking back, he wished she had stayed away, then maybe he could have forgotten that he even had a mother, or he could have made up a story about her leaving and wanting to reach out to him but not being able to. Like Old Min and his daughter. His teacher had spent years looking for his daughter; they were not together, but his love for her was still there. JJ thought about how Old Min's daughter would react upon receiving her father's ashes.

Sitting up on his bed, JJ reached for his luggage. He dived a hand inside and rummaged deep within as he peered out the porthole. His hand reached the bottom of the luggage, but he still could not find what he was searching for. He was expecting his fingers to brush against the soft silk of the scarf that wrapped around Old Min's urn, but there was nothing. He pulled his luggage closer and started taking his belongings out, one by one, becoming more frantic with each item he removed. Once JJ frantically emptied his luggage, he sat back, his shoulders slumped. He had no choice but to confront the reality: the urn was gone.

# Chapter 5

JJ rushed out of the cabin to look for Fred. He was not on the ship deck where JJ had left him. Even though it was too early for lunch, he went to the dining hall, as he knew Fred liked to bother the waitresses while they prepared for the midday service. But the hall was empty. He ran to the smoking room, the cinema, the billiard room, and still no sign of Fred. He did not see Marcel either.

He could not believe someone had taken the urn, but where was it? Back in the cabin, he rummaged through his belongings again. This time, he found a small piece of folded paper. He opened it and read it. It looked like a clue to a treasure hunt.

*Rub away, if you must. Let me collect all that dust. Just stomp away, I never hide. I keep the outdoors away from the inside.*

Fred! He was the only one who knew about the jar, and nobody else would come up with such an idea.

JJ frowned, thinking that the last time he took part in a treasure hunt was with George, a couple of years after JJ first arrived in Phnom Penh. They had been visiting a large house, with a garden at least twice as big as theirs and a swimming pool in the middle of a lawn of emerald grass cut so low, no snakes could have gone unnoticed. Several families gathered for Easter, and the children were told to search the painted eggs. Screaming with joy, the young ones had dashed outside to the garden, excited by the granted freedom, but as soon as they were told the eggs were hidden in the house, they sat on the stairs with long faces as they knew that they were not allowed to run and scream inside. George, meanwhile, was excited and started running all over the house to look for the eggs. JJ trailed behind him, curious to see the eggs.

When they found the first one, George shouted, 'Look, I've found a blue one!'

JJ approached and together they looked at the blue eggshell with yellow dots.

'JJ, you could have painted these eggs much better,' George said.

'How did they paint it? Let me have a look,' JJ said, stretching out his hand for the egg, but George kept it in his hand.

'Wait, do you think it is coloured inside too?' George asked.

'Why would it be?'

'The egg is hard-boiled. Maybe they boiled it with colour. Like the eggs they sell at the market. They are not white, they are brown,' George answered.

'We could open it,' JJ suggested, his tone uncertain.

'But then we will lose one point,' George said. 'The lady told us there is a prize for those who find the most eggs.'

'You are right. But I am not sure I want a prize from them,' JJ said, thinking how the two children of the house used to bully others.

'C'est pour ça! That's why… we must find more eggs than the others, to show that they are not better than us,' George said.

'Wait, I have a better idea. I have my colours here with me. We could get some eggs from the kitchen, paint them, and put them in the basket,' JJ said, surprising himself with his boldness.

George jumped around with glee and instead of egg hunting, they ended up having a good time trying to steal eggs from the busy kitchen. When JJ's father got wind of their plan, he sent them to a corner, shaming them in front of the other children. George and JJ were having such a good time, though, that they kept laughing in their corner.

The current hunt for the urn, however, did not make JJ laugh. He felt hopeless despite the clue he held in his hand, he had no idea what it meant. The more he read the note, the redder and warmer he felt his face becoming. He jumped down to the floor and darted for the door, running so suddenly into Marcel as he entered the cabin. Marcel held JJ by the shoulders to prevent him from stumbling.

'Where is your stupid brother?' JJ spat out the words before he registered what he had said.

Marcel looked at JJ's swollen face and shallow breathing. 'What did my brother do? I knew the lad would bring me trouble.' Marcel poured a glass of water and handed it to JJ, whose face slowly returned to its usual colour. 'I should not have taken him with me. I'll show him how to behave.'

Back to his usual quiet self, JJ took another sip.

'So, tell me, what did my brother do?' Marcel asked again.

'Nothing, it is not so important. I am being silly. We are playing a treasure hunt and I am not good at it,' JJ said.

Marcel raised an eyebrow, unconvinced by JJ's explanation. He noticed the slip of paper in JJ's hand and asked to see it.

'Indeed, it looks like a clue,' Marcel said. *Rub away, if you must. Let me collect all that dust. Just stomp away, I never hide. I keep the outdoors away from the inside.*'

Marcel sat still for a few minutes, then passed the note back to JJ. 'Sorry, kid. The only treasure hunts I've been on involved searching for whisky and women. I'm not good at this either. Try to ask that French family from Lyon we met on the deck once; they have kids.'

JJ took the note and left the cabin, his back slightly arched.

Marcel sat down on his berth and while he untied his shoes to lie down, he saw a pile of clothes on JJ's berth.

A short time later, the cabin door opened, and Fred stepped in with his usual vigour, finding Marcel in bed. Before he could retreat, his brother sat up.

'So, what's the story with JJ?' Marcel asked Fred, his tone deep and slow. 'He looked very upset.'

Fred's energy dissipated and clumsily, he said he did not know.

'What's the treasure hunt?' Marcel asked.

'Ah, nothing. We are just playing,' Fred said, turning to leave. 'I will go look for him.'

His brother stood up and stopped him. 'You might think you are playing, but JJ was not game. What did you take from him?'

'Take? Me? Nothing,' Fred said, his chest rising as he gave Marcel his best innocent look, which always worked with his mother.

Marcel's fist hit the desk, emitting a loud thwack. 'Don't you lie to me. I hate lies. If you feel old enough to be a scoundrel, then own up to it and have the courage to say so when asked.'

Fred stood still, looking at his brother, barely daring to breathe.

'Don't look at me like a rabbit. I asked you a

question.' Marcel paced around the cabin. 'We are not even in China yet and you are already making trouble. Look at you, I bet you want to piss in your pants.'

Marcel approached his brother and brought his face a few centimetres from Fred's face. 'What did you take from him? This is the last time I ask you,' Marcel said between his teeth, his voice was now a whisper.

'A… a small jar. It is not valuable. It is just a joke,' Fred said, his small Adam's apple going up and down.

'Where is this jar now?' Marcel asked.

'I hid it in one of my boots,' Fred said, separating each word slowly, as if the sentence required an amount of air he did not have.

'Now, you take it out and put it back where it was. And I want you to fold all his clothes and repack his luggage nicely,' Marcel said. He then returned to his berth and lay down with his eyes closed, and Fred knew his brother was sure he would comply with his orders.

*\*\*\**

After leaving the cabin, JJ walked towards the laundry room, resisting the urge to cry along the way. He opened the door to find two women busy chatting while they folded their clothing. He stepped back and walked to his usual corner on the lower deck, where he sat on a chair, taking his head in his hands. He felt cold at the thought of having caused Fred trouble with his brother. He replayed the scene over and over in his mind, trying to convince himself that he did not give away what Fred had done. But the urn. Where was it? Was its lid still sealed? He started trembling and finally the tears he had restrained so far flowed down his face.

He didn't know how long he had stayed there, but his

face was dry when Fred found him. He sprang up from his seat as Fred gave him a tense smile.

'I'm sorry, JJ. I put all your clothes and the jar back in your luggage,' Fred said.

'What about the lid, is it still there?'

'Yes, of course. I did not open it. I tried, though…' Fred said, thinking about what his brother told him, 'but I did not want to break it.'

JJ sighed with relief, his hands in front of his chest as if in prayer. 'You scared me to death. You don't know what this jar is.'

'I would be glad to know, but you never told me when I asked you about it.'

'Well, it is personal,' JJ said.

'But are we not friends? Friends should not have secrets,' Fred said, annoyed.

'It's my teacher.'

'What?' Fred was so loud, his voice chased away a couple of birds that had landed on the ship when they had docked.

'The jar is an urn, and it contains the ashes of my teacher. I have to bring them to his daughter in China,' JJ said. 'And there is more.' He also told Fred about Old Min's letter and the mission his teacher had supposedly charged him with.

'So, you are not sure the letter comes from your teacher?' Fred asked him after hearing the story.

'I am not sure, but who else could have written it and why?' JJ said, then regretted the question; Fred would likely come up with the most fantastical stories about the letter, which would not bring him closer to the truth.

'He asked one of the nurses,' Fred simply said.

JJ looked surprised by the suggestion.

'Sure, my father did the same. I once had a terrible

44

school report... well, not only once, but that year was particularly bad. My father was in a hospital far away from home and was quite debilitated. But my mother insisted that he write a letter to me with all sorts of threats, to put me back on the right path, so his nurse wrote the letter under his dictation and then he signed it.'

'I never thought about that,' JJ said. 'Yes. That could be it.' JJ then hit his forehead with his hand. 'This means I have to accept his mission. Oh my gosh, how will I do it?'

Fred rejoiced. 'I knew there was an adventure awaiting us!'

*** 

Over the next weeks, the deceptive sea, which had so far fooled the *Cambodge* passengers, became tired of the pleasant roll of the ship and decided to swirl. The skies agreed, and soon the thunder and crashing waves were all the passengers could see and hear, leaving more than one fighting to keep their food down.

Lying in his berth, JJ leaned over to check on his new friend. 'Fred, are you still seasick? Do you want to eat something?'

'I'm fine, but I am not sure I want to eat breakfast after what happened last time I tried to eat.'

'The sea seems to be calmer than yesterday,' JJ pointed out.

'It is true. Where are we?' Fred asked, trying in vain to get a glimpse out of the porthole.

'I think we are approaching the Strait of Malacca,' JJ said, getting up and peering at the sea from the porthole.

'The Strait of Malacca? I've heard that many ships sink in this area.'

45

'Don't you worry. The ship's cruising speed has decreased as well. I am sure nothing will happen.'

'I am not worried,' Fred replied. 'I'm only wondering about all the forgotten treasures deep in the sea.'

'Alright, sounds like you are feeling better, then,' JJ said. 'Let's go to breakfast.'

'I don't want to go. Last time it was not very edible anyway,' Fred said with a yawn.

JJ climbed onto his bed to put his sketchbook back in his luggage. 'I think they are running out of supplies; I overheard one waiter complaining about the extra food and service the politician and his delegation expect.'

'Not us, we are in the delegation, but we don't get even an additional slice of bread. We have not once been invited to the first-class dining hall,' Fred huffed, crossing his arms on his chest. When he saw JJ climbing down, he asked, 'Your teacher still fine? Not too dull in there?'

'I just put my sketchbook back. The urn is still there, yes,' JJ said with a little smile. Even in his grief for his teacher, he found Fred's comments funny.

'He is a quiet companion,' Fred said.

'And he doesn't take too much space,' JJ said.

They both laughed, then Fred asked what the next stop was, and he got up to look at the itinerary map, which he had hung on the cabin's wall.

'Singapore,' Fred said, 'and then Saigon, yes. We are getting there, my friend. Welcome to the French colony. Indochina.' His eyes sparkled with pleasure, and he whistled as he got dressed to join JJ for breakfast.

# Chapter 6

By the time the *Cambodge* reached Saigon, the two friends had a routine. They stood outside on the deck and scanned the approaching shore, taking in the buildings of the Dragon Wharf, the Saigon harbour.

'We are here! Saigon,' Fred said, his voice excited. 'My brother once had a pal who served here, and he told me all about it. People say the city is a beauty, with large boulevards like in Paris, and the theatre building is a copy of the Paris Petit Palais.'

Fred offered JJ the binoculars, which he got from his brother after nagging him to death, but JJ shook his head and sat on one of the deck chairs.

'Oh my... your mood is even worse than the time I woke you up at three am to see Colombo from a distance.'

'I am not in a bad mood. It is just that I am not interested,' he replied, but instead of resuming the drawing he was working on before Fred snatched the sketchbook from his hands, he just stared into the void.

Fred glimpsed his friend's tense face, but his attention soon turned to the activity on the pier. 'Look, JJ, the army unit is disembarking. I wonder where they will go first. With such a heat, that must not be easy marching around, I don't envy them,' he said, taking another glimpse at the departing troops. 'Good luck, my friends, good luck.'

Fred sighed softly, 'I cannot believe that we might lose our colonies in Indochina!' He leaned over the railing, contorting his body to the right and to the left.

'Damn, we cannot see much of the city from here. I would love to get off the ship. What a pity we are not allowed to leave the ship. I see a tall building there, look. Maybe it's the rooftop of the theatre… I am sure it is!'

'Which one? The one with the two towers? No, of course it is not. It's the Notre-Dame Cathedral,' JJ said, still sitting in his chair.

'How can you say that?' Fred asked, turning to JJ with an interrogating look. 'You don't even know which building I am talking about.'

'I just know,' he said and this time he took his sketchbook in his hands again.

'Well, you may think what you want, but I say that it is the theatre building. It looks like that to me,' Fred said, leaning further from the railing.

'I know which building you mean. I've seen it before,' JJ said in a flat tone. 'I lived in Indochina during the war. My father had a post in Cambodia.'

Fred gasped and looked at him with wide eyes. 'What… what?' he said, 'You lived in Indochina? For how long?'

'About four years.'

'Four years? Why you didn't say anything?' said Fred, both surprised and fired up.

'I didn't feel like talking about it.'

'How often must I have made foolish comments about the colonies, while you knew better,' he said, hitting his forehead with his hand.

'I did not mind listening to your stories. This is what friends do, isn't it?' JJ said, looking at Fred's face. He felt relieved to see that his friend was not upset.

'You must tell me everything now. You have been in Saigon and where else? What was your house like? How many domestics did you have?'

'I just told you. My father had a post in the administration. We lived in Phnom Penh.'

'Phnom Penh? How was it, like Saigon? Bigger?'

'No.'

'What did you eat?'

'Bread.'

'Bread? There was bread?' he asked, astonished. 'And wine? How large was the house?'

'Four rooms.'

'Where did you sleep? Did you have a mosquito net? And a fan, I guess?'

'Yes.'

'How were the people? Could they understand you? How did you go around?'

'I stayed at home.'

'Did you taste anything weird? A monkey or so?'

'Fred, Fred, stop it! I don't want to talk about that time. I was unhappy, and it has no meaning for me. I don't want to think about it. Stop your questioning! And Fred, you can't tell anyone.'

'What, but why? Such a great experience, even my brother might be envious.'

'I can't explain why, but I don't feel comfortable talking about it. Please, please, we are friends, aren't we? You are my friend.'

'Okay, okay, but you have to tell me at least about Saigon!'

'There is nothing to say,' JJ said. 'It's a city with a couple of nice buildings, lots of Asians, and very far from France.'

Fred was not convinced. JJ put his hands in his trouser pockets but felt Fred's eyes looking at him, full of reproach. JJ got up and returned to the lounge, where the presence of other people would hinder Fred from asking him more questions.

JJ did not see Fred the rest of the day, and when he joined their usual table at dinner, he found Fred sitting at the other end, next to the wall, with no seat available near him.

Marcel asked if they fought again, eyeing his brother.

'No. JJ seems to be bothered by my company, so I guess he prefers to be alone,' Fred said, sipping his soup loudly.

Marcel just shook his head without further comment, while JJ felt his limbs go cold. He ate his cordon bleu in silence and waited for Fred to get up to go after him.

'Fred, I do enjoy your company. It is just… that part of my life is painful to remember. Let's go upstairs, shall we?' JJ said and led his friend to their favourite spot on the deck above the dining hall.

'There is not much to say,' JJ started. They sat on deck chairs and JJ continued, 'We had arrived on a similar ship, before the war broke out in Europe. My father had accepted a post here. I guess he thought it would be safer for us. And also, that it could help his career. We took the train to get to Phnom Penh, where we stayed almost all the time. My mother loved Saigon at first and we had been there a few times at the beginning, maybe one time around Christmas. But once she settled in Phnom Penh, she didn't insist on going to Saigon that much.' JJ took a couple of deep breaths. 'Yes, Saigon was beautiful, and strange. All these men in white uniforms and all others looking so dark in comparison. I hated the confusion. I hated those people who stared and pointed at me, as if I were a monster. I mostly stayed at home, in my room, and spent my time drawing.' *Or with George*, he thought.

'Did you go to school there, then?' Fred asked.

'I had a private tutor. My mother was also teaching me some… I could seldom leave the house. I would see people only when my parents held a dinner party, and that was quite regularly.' There have been so many parties that he could only remember a few, like the one when he got sick.

That day, as preparations for an evening party were keeping the servants busy in the house, JJ and George were left to play in the garden with little supervision. On their knees, they were looking at something as JJ heard his mother shouting that she was home. A short while after, she appeared in the back garden.

'Mes enfants, what are you looking at?' she asked.

George got up and answered with his usual enthusiasm. 'Bonjour, Aunt Suzanne, you are beautiful as ever,' and he threw his arms around JJ's mother, leading JJ to wonder why his cousin was so fond of her. Next to his cousin, who was tall for his age, his mother still looked like a giant, and there was no mistake where JJ took his slender frame from. Her blue eyes strangely matched George's, a colour JJ often tried to reproduce in his drawing.

'Look, Aunty, JJ and I collected some leaves and flowers, and we are making a wreath,' George said, while JJ was still absorbed in arranging the leaves according to their shade of colour.

'Very nice,' she said, giving him a smile and turning to JJ.

'Jeanou, we have guests tonight. I'm going to take a bath, and you can take yours in half an hour. The maid will leave your outfit for tonight on your bed. D'accord, chéri?'

JJ looked briefly at her without replying.

She turned to George.

'Is your driver coming to pick you up?'

George shrugged. 'I don't know.'

'Does your mother know you are here at all?' she asked, looking straight into his eyes.

'I don't know,' he said, opening his hands as if to show that he was not guilty of anything.

'Alright, whatever. If nobody shows up, you can stay for dinner. But don't forget to wash your hands before coming to the table.'

When she turned and went inside, JJ followed quietly a few steps behind her. He wanted to ask if he could eat in his room. He stopped short when he saw that she had bumped into his father.

'You are back. I'll be ready in one hour. Our son is outside with George,' his mother said. While she had lost weight since they got there, he looked like he had put some on. His brown beard had been cleanly trimmed a few days ago, and he looked distinguished in his three-piece suit, which compensated for his plain face. She was the beauty of the family, the prize he won with marriage, and even though she was not too bothered by his ugliness, his mother often told him she was glad to see that her Jeanou took after her.

'Are the kitchen maid's little bastards also there?' his father asked.

'No, it's only JJ and George. Why?'

'You know I don't like our son playing with them. They are taking advantage of him,' his father said, striding into the spacious living room, where the maid just left a drink for him.

'Maybe, but JJ is so lonely. George does not come often enough,' his mother said, following him.

'Not sure George is the right company, either. What are they doing outside?' He took a sip of his mango juice with grenadine. 'Any chance they are torturing a bird?'

'You know our son would never be so cruel. He gets upset so easily. They are making a wreath of leaves and flowers,' she said, and she set out towards the bedroom.

From a distance, his father's words could still be heard, a loud sneer accompanying the words that wreaths were a girly occupation.

From the corner where JJ had hidden himself, he wondered why his father did not like the children of the maid or George, and thought it was so difficult to please him. He waited for his father to retreat to his study, then JJ joined his mother. He knocked on the bedroom door.

'Maman, can I eat in the room? I don't feel well today.'

'What is it, Jeanou? You know your father prefers that we all eat together.' His mother was busy searching in her wardrobe, and she was not looking at him.

'What can I wear? They all look so old... If I wear the black one, I will be a laughingstock. Nobody wears black here. It is just white, white, white... awful colour. It does not go well with my skin,' she said, looking at her wardrobe, her hands on her hips.

'Maman... '

'Oui, mon chéri?' she replied, still turning her back on him.

His mother had already forgotten his question, and he looked at her dispirited.

She turned and in three steps she reached her toilet table, from where she grabbed a box, took two pills and swallowed them with a glass of water. He often saw her taking pills.

'Are you sick?' he asked.

'My head hurts.' She finally turned her attention to him. 'You look fine to me, Jeanou. Don't always find excuses. I told you I have a headache. You are already making my head worse, and I don't want to add listening to your father's comments on top of that.'

JJ wanted to ask which comments, but his mother gestured at him to leave the room.

'You go and change. Be a good boy, Jeanou, oui?'

He left, once again rejected by his mother, and with the feeling of being responsible for making his mother sick. With a long face, he went to his room to change, unaware that being sick could sometimes turn into a blessing, as he discovered after the outcome of the evening.

# Chapter 7

That night, his mother wore a simple, long dress and JJ thought she looked very pretty. Her eyes were not so red, as they were sometimes. But her cheeks were red; she had put some powder or similar stuff on them to make them look so. At nine, JJ was faintly aware that when she put red on her cheeks, many men were coming for dinner.

At the table, she laughed and laughed. She did not even notice that JJ was not eager to eat. The maid gave him for dinner a large portion of potage aux crevettes, a soup with those funny pink fish. His mother knew that he did not eat that. But she did not look at him, and she did not come to his rescue when his father urged him to finish his dish. JJ lowered his head, hoping at least that his father would forget about him too, and not ask JJ to go with him and his friends to his studio.

'JJ, come join us. We're going for one last drink. Come, my son, don't sit there like a sissy.'

JJ pushed his chair out, scraping its legs along the floor, to clear enough space from the table to stand up.

A man gave JJ a long stare while they were walking towards his father's studio, the room of hell.

'So, this is your son, Monsieur Leduc? He looks like a fine boy.' He bent his head towards JJ. 'How does our little boy like living in the colony?'

JJ only looked back at this man. He was ancient, with a white beard.

'JJ, respond to the question,' he heard his father

saying.

'I prefer living in France,' JJ answered.

His father's voice came as fast as thunder. 'Well, you are here now, and you better get used to it. Serve our guests a glass of cognac.' His father turned to the ancient man, but JJ felt his eyes on his back. 'This boy lacks character, wastes all his time in the house.'

'Yes, his mother told me at dinner that he spends all his time drawing.'

'He doesn't have a clue about life. At his age I was already a grown little man, helping my father in his business.'

JJ brought each guest a glass with the right amount of cognac, the smell of alcohol making him sick in the stomach. He fought back the impulse to throw up his soup.

'His mother too thinks he is so childish,' his father said as he took his glass, giving his son a disapproving look.

JJ could not hold the feeling in anymore. He pitched forward and vomited on his father's shoes.

At the end of JJ's story, Fred laughed so hard that two passengers chatting nearby gave them a hard look.

'What did your father then do?' Fred asked.

'He sent me to my room and did not allow me to have dinner with the family for one week.' JJ grinned. 'It was great. I could stay in my room and draw as much as I wanted.'

It was the first time JJ realised he remembered so much. Memories kept pouring forth like monsoon rains. He could recollect tiny details and fragments of conversations; he could see that his stories excited Fred, so JJ kept telling him more, eager to make his friend happy. But he still could not bring himself to tell that last story and only offered less painful ones.

'I was sometimes included in the company of the gentlemen. My father thought it could teach me something despite my young age. I cared little about their discussions and only much later I understood the meaning of some conversations.'

'What were they talking about? War?' Fred asked.

'Well, there was a bit of everything. War, of course, but also gossip.' JJ poured himself a glass of water from the jug they had brought out from the dining hall. 'Once an officer told a story about a country girl, not so young and not pretty,' he said. 'She was at the market bargaining with a merchant about the price of vegetables. They were louder than the usual tone Asians have when talking to each other, and a guard intervened. When the girl was asked what her job was, she replied, 'Spouse of foreigners.' At that point of the story, the officer and everybody else in the room started laughing.' JJ could see that his friend was not sure whether he was now supposed to laugh too.

Fred then ventured to ask, 'Why did the girl say that? Was she married to a foreigner?'

'No, not at all. I only understood later what she meant. She was a domestic helper assigned to the household of an officer. There were always officers coming and going, staying a few months there, then leaving for another post. Each officer would get a housing; a servant warming the bed was part of the benefits many officers enjoyed.'

Fred remained speechless for a moment. 'What else? What else?' he urged JJ.

'Well, nothing else. They had these kinds of conversations. They also gossiped about who was regularly going to the opium den, who slept with whom... Nothing was ever openly said, but after a few of these conversations you would grasp the code they used.'

'Have you been to the theatre in Saigon?'

'I have been only once. There was an opera or something. Not much difference from any other opera in France, except that only the main singers were Europeans and there were lots of Asian faces on stage.'

Another flashback hit JJ: a rich plantation owner insulting and spitting on a rickshaw driver, because he had accidentally splashed pond water on the rich man's coat while passing by.

Another flashback. A Japanese soldier shooting a young boy who had stolen what was left in a bowl of rice. JJ's mother had covered his eyes with her hands, but JJ had still glimpsed through her fingers the blood that spilled from the boy's body. He asked himself how a tiny boy could have had so much blood in his frail body, which was so thin that bones were sticking out.

Fred saw his friend grow silent and his eyes darken. He felt somewhat envious. He used to dream about pirates and adventures in faraway lands but his life up to that day had been dull and uneventful, his mother constantly behind him stuffing him like a turkey and taking his hand everywhere they went. During the war, he was too young and the resistance movement in his town did not accept him. His brother, on the other hand, spent some time in the Legion of Honour and then joined a resistance group, which oversaw the liaison with army units in the UK.

When Fred heard that Marcel was going to China for business, he pestered his brother to take him along and cajoled his mother to plead Marcel on his behalf. This was his first opportunity to leave France and to have, finally, the adventures he longed for. Marcel treated him more like a stranger than a brother, but to Fred, he was someone to emulate. He told himself that of course Marcel was so smart and brave; he was a good ten years older than Fred and he had left home early. But now, he left home too.

Fred shook his head at JJ. 'If I were you, I would have spent every single moment outside. So, you were friends with other kids, you said?'

JJ pinched his lips together, pouting. 'They were not my friends. Only George was my real friend. Once he lied to my father to cover for me because by mistake, I had spilled watercolours on a record my father loved.'

'But did you not say that a maid's kids played with you?'

'Yes, but they were not my friends. They just wanted to get something from me.'

'Like what?'

'Like food or small gifts, whatever. But especially food. They often showed up shortly before goûter and as the maid was preparing an afternoon snack for me, I would always ask them to stay.'

'But this does not mean they were not friends.'

JJ got up and clenched his hands on his knees. 'They were not my friends. My father said so, and I also heard my mother saying that to my aunt. I was just a stupid kid. I understood that later. But no wonder that my mother did not like me.' JJ relaxed his body a little and said, 'Yes, my only two friends had been George and Old Min.'

'How did you meet your teacher? You never told me the whole story,' Fred asked.

'Old Min moved into the flat above ours in the 15ème arrondissment in 1951.' It was the same year General Petain died, and the radio kept retelling his life story. JJ could clearly remember that he was trying to get on paper the nuances of an orchid when his mother came into his room to tell him that an Asian man was moving in above them. She seemed thrilled.

'I could not talk to him right away,' she had said, 'as he was busy with the movers, but he can speak French. I wonder where he is from… Oh, I can never really tell the difference between Asians. I think we should invite him here. What do you think, Jeanou?'

JJ looked at his mother, still shocked to see her hair cut so short. He was not the only one; his father had been furious.

'If you want,' JJ replied. 'But he won't like your cooking. He is Asian.'

'Mon Jeanou, there are many Asians who like French cuisine. All our guests back in Phnom Penh always appreciated our dinners.'

He could see his mother drifting back to old memories, to warm and humid nights spent with the most implausible friends, whose only thing in common was sharing the boredom of being stuck in the same city.

JJ met Old Min a few days later as JJ returned from a class. Opening the main door, he found the hall full of bonsai, maybe fifteen or so. Old Min was coming down the stairs wearing dark trousers, too large for his body, and a white-and-grey chunky checked shirt, which hung out of his trousers untucked. His white hair matched the colour of a few hairs he had under his chin. He greeted JJ with a bonjour, eating up his 'r' like many Asians did. He lifted two bonsai and headed upstairs.

Without being asked, JJ picked up two as well and shouted at his neighbour's back that he could help him. Old Min replied with a smile and many thanks. They walked up and down the stairs a few times, in silence.

Once all the bonsai were in the flat, Old Min offered JJ a cup of Iron Buddha tea, a green tea JJ would discover his teacher was fond of. The flat was not very spacious, but it had a large balcony, or at least it seemed large before all the bonsai took their residence there. It now looked like a mini jungle. The living room had a worn-out leather couch, and on the walls, JJ saw several scrolls of a regular scribble. Old Min was apparently their author as next to the window, there was a table with brushes of different sizes, ink, and sheets of thin paper, some of which were as scribbled on as the scrolls.

'Chinese calligraphy. You know Chinese calligraphy?'

JJ shook his head.

'No? Ancient art, me many many years practise, good for the mind, nourish the spirit. What you do? Student?'

'Yes, I study arts in the académie.'

'Oh, arts very good very good. You need do calligraphy then, calligraphy difficult art, very nice.' Old Min went to the table and spread out a white sheet of paper. He raised his arm and motioned for JJ to join him by swinging his hand back-and-forth palm down. He poured a few drops of black ink onto a black stone with a slight hollow. He prepared the ink, then he showed JJ how to hold the brush and to move it carefully on the paper, his arm floating in the air while writing. Old Min traced a long, sinuous black line, from top to bottom, without removing the tip of his brush from the paper until he added a few shorter strokes on the side.

'永 yǒng. Forever.'

He made JJ copy the character on another sheet, once, twice, and again. They carried on for half an hour, side by side, in silence. When it came time for JJ to leave,

Old Min told him:

'You come day after tomorrow, afternoon, yes? We practise good. Thank you. Goodbye.' And he closed the door without waiting for an answer.

JJ stood outside, unsure what to make of his invitation. Descending the stairs to go back home, he asked himself whether he really expected him to visit him again.

# Chapter 8

Two days later, JJ rang the bell at Old Min's door. His neighbour answered with a curt nod, then led him to the table. Paper, ink, and brush were waiting. Old Min drew a character.

'Voilà, now you copy. Copy many time, oui?' Old Min said.

Thus, without having asked or expressed any wish to learn Chinese calligraphy, JJ found himself as Old Min's pupil. He visited Old Min twice or three times a week. Old Min would show him the character to learn and leave JJ to practise alone, while he went to the balcony to take care of his bonsais. For each character, Old Min also taught him the pronunciation and the meaning.

| 口 | *kǒu* | mouth |
|---|---|---|
| 人 | *rén* | person |
| 大 | *dà* | large |
| 天 | *tiān* | day |

But the second time JJ wrote the character, Old Min added a new meaning.

| | | |
|---|---|---|
| 口 | *kǒu* | opening |
| 人 | *rén* | adult |
| 大 | *dà* | strong |
| 天 | *tiān* | God |

JJ became fascinated by the multiple meanings and the deceiving simplicity of the calligraphy, and thus he practised diligently every week. At the end of each session, Old Min would approach and look at the sheet, then he would take a brush and mark the mistakes with red ink. They would not talk a lot at the beginning, each absorbed in his own occupation. There was, nevertheless a placid atmosphere, a harmonious feeling that spread from each corner of the flat. JJ could not grasp what created this atmosphere as the flat was chock-full of stuff: a small altar, normal-sized plants, books, a tea set with several tiny cups, and a bin that was conveniently next to the side table to throw the old tea leaves from the teapot.

He realised only later that the flat was quite tidy; there was not a piece of old paper in sight, for example, and he could not see any cluttered corner or any drawer where odd things usually landed, as in many households. He was especially intrigued because practising calligraphy required lots of paper. He asked Old Min once where all the sheets of paper went.

'Thrown. Have many old things no good. Bad fēngshuǐ. Bad yuánfèn, or how you call it? Karma? Me, enough bad karma. Lived places where no choice. Door wrong. Bed wrong, but no possible change. Now I choose, no bad karma more. I live with peace.'

'Where is your family?' JJ ventured to ask.

'Family China, left many years ago. Me come to France, get money, and send home. But home too difficult, war with Japanese, war with Guómíndǎng, the Nationalists, no good. Long-time lost contacts, no see family. Wife, small baby. Asked friend to see but could not find, too much disorder, no law is clear. Today is this law, tomorrow is this law. Bad time, very sad. Friend find wife die, daughter somewhere else. No found my daughter more.'

Involuntarily JJ's eyes moved towards the small altar, where a picture of a middle-aged lady was standing among short tea candles.

'My wife here, she French. No picture my Chinese wife or baby. They picture in my heart only,' Old Min added, noticing the direction of JJ's gaze.

***

Fred whistled in awe. 'Wow, Old Min must also have had an adventurous life,' he said. 'And he had two wives, good for him.' Fred was pleased about his comment, which was like those his brother seemed to make.

JJ and Fred felt a warm breeze through their light shirts as the evenings had got more humid since they passed the Strait of Malacca. Fred got up from his seat and paced around while JJ remained sitting on the reclining deck chair.

'JJ, I was thinking. You will stay in China for a while, right? What if I take the scroll with me back to France and sell it for you?' Fred asked. He had been thinking about this for a while and thought he could show his brother what he was capable of.

'Really? Do you think you can do it?'

'Of course, why not?' Fred reasoned that if the scroll was truly from a famous painter, then he should be able to sell it without too much trouble. 'I can send you the money and you can give it to your teacher's daughter.'

'Yes, that might be workable. What if we discuss it with your brother, though?'

Fred rolled his eyes and looked at JJ with his arms crossed. 'You think I cannot do it?'

JJ rushed to reassure him. 'I do, but your brother has more contacts and experience. You know that I can't make a mistake here.'

Fred knew his friend was right, but he did not want to leave the matter in his brother's hands.

'Alright, what about this? We ask my brother in general terms, like, what to do when selling art. What do you think?'

'Okay, we can do that,' JJ said.

'No, I do that. You leave it to me, alright?' Fred said, pressing his palm on his shirt. He looked at the city lights far on the horizon. 'What a pity we cannot get off,' he lamented.

'We will arrive in Hong Kong soon. Maybe you will have time there. We have a few hours to change the ship,' JJ said.

'Yes,' Fred said, rubbing his hands. 'I will be the first to fly off the boat.'

They spent the next few days reading an old book by a Spanish novelist, who wrote about this journey around the word. JJ and Fred found a copy of the second volume, where the novelist recounted his adventures in Hong Kong and China, among others. Fred complained that the book was old, but the reading still kept them busy until the ship finally reached the British colony.

On the day the ship pulled closer to Hong Kong, the two friends leaned against the parapet to look out. Since they had crossed the Strait of Malacca, endless junks hugged the coastline and kept the *Cambodge* company all the way to British colony.

'This is what I call a sight. It reminds me of the agricultural fair this year,' Fred said.

'Why? Were there any junks there?'

'No, but it was full of tractors. All shapes, colours, large, small, for one person, or for the whole family,' Fred said. 'Look there. That junk is so heavy with goods that the water is just a few centimetres from the edge. If someone on the deck jumps, the water will get in for sure,' he added with a laugh. 'I would not like to be in one of those,' he continued, unaware of what the future had in store for them.

'Yes, they use the junks for everything. Some families live on them. Look at that one, the smaller one with two sails. The lady is doing the laundry at the back.'

'They live on the boat? Always?' Fred asked.

'Yes, they only leave it to buy supplies.'

'And where do they… Aaah, I don't want to know,' he said, looking at the brownish water, the corners of his mouth turning downwards.

The ship proceeded in an irregular zigzag amid the deserted, hilly islets and the larger islands.

'It is taking forever to reach the harbour. These islets seem to grow out of nothing,' JJ said. 'After we pass one, here comes another.'

'You are right. Let's bet whether we'll see a junk, an island, or the harbour after the next turn.'

'Oh, why not? I bet five francs that at the next turn, we see an island.'

'Five francs? You are stingy. You can barely buy bread with that. I bet fifty francs that at the next turn, we see… another junk,' Fred said.

'Fifty? No, no, I can go only up to ten francs.'

'A glass of wine? Okay, better than bread.' Fred laughed.

Their betting game went on for almost one hour before they finally glimpsed Victoria Harbour. The ship navigated the narrow sea space between the Kowloon Peninsula and Hong Kong Island, offering passengers a view of several modern buildings, including a tall skyscraper towering in the distance. Both sides of the harbour were busy: ships, junks, and ferries, each claiming their own space in the crowded waters. Above, a few clouds, which shrouded the peaks beyond the buildings south of the harbour, accompanied the blue sky.

They docked on the island side and had almost the whole day to change ship and board another that would take them to Shanghai. The transfer took less than two hours for the Maréchal brothers and JJ, who all shared a cabin again, albeit a much smaller one with a tiny porthole, which let little sea breeze in. Outside, the air was sticky, despite the temperature being about eighteen degrees.

'Fred, this time you stay on board,' Marcel told his brother.

Fred's mouth was agape. 'What? Why?'

'You heard what the Englishman said about the shantytown near the border and the Chinese refugees. He said that some boarded the ships to steal from the passengers' cabins. I need you to keep an eye on the luggage.'

'Why don't you stay here then?'

'Because I am busy. One of the Englishmen gave me the address of a few silk shops and a presentation letter for the owner of one import-export company. I want to check it out before we leave for China,' Marcel said.

'Well, JJ never leaves the ship. He can help look after the luggage, can't you, JJ?' Fred said, with an imploring look at JJ and his brother. He would have liked to go around Hong Kong with JJ, as he noticed how difficult it was to move around speaking only French, but if he had to choose between staying on the ship or disembarking, he would sacrifice JJ's company.

To Fred's relief, JJ eagerly agreed to stay on board and watch their belongings.

Fred saw his brother's eyes narrow as they looked straight at him. When he spoke, his tone was deeper than usual. 'Fred, this is our luggage. You look after it.' Marcel turned to JJ and said in his normal tone, 'JJ, you don't have to stay here with Fred. Leave the ship if you want.'

Marcel took money from the interior pocket of his luggage, put it between the pages of his passport, and left the two friends alone in the cabin.

'If you leave the ship without me, I'll kill you,' Fred said. He unbuttoned the collar and the cuffs of his shirt in a vain attempt to cool his body with fresh air. He grumbled to himself in a low voice and got louder after a few minutes. 'This is not acceptable. How can he do that to me? He is going on land to have fun, and I am imprisoned on this ship.'

Fred looked at his friend, who sat in silence listening to him. His quietness irritated Fred, and he complained about his brother even louder, making it impossible for JJ to ignore him.

'Tell me, JJ, do you really think my brother has the right to tell me what to do? Am I not old enough to decide?'

Instead of giving a reply, JJ got up to go to the toilet. When he came back, Fred had JJ's diary in his hand.

'How can you write in such a crisis?' Fred said, glaring at his friend. In a rage, he threw JJ's diary at a wall.

'Hey, don't do that!' JJ said, reaching for his diary.

Fred was not placated, and he swiftly picked up the diary and ripped out the last page. He tore it in half and was about to shred it into smaller pieces when he heard a loud cry of agony from JJ. He watched as JJ fell to his knees, picked up the torn pieces, and tried to piece them together.

'He was my cousin, he was my cousin,' JJ said, tears streaming down his face. 'You don't know what you have done. You don't know what I have done.'

# Chapter 9

'JJ, what is it? Why the hell are you crying like this?' Fred asked, placing his hands in his pockets while he bent forward towards JJ, who was still on the floor holding the scraps of paper.

'I do not have any other drawing of George. I lost his picture. Without the drawing, I won't remember what he looks like,' JJ replied, his tears escaping like thick drops of oil. 'I must not forget him, ever, after what I did.'

'What did you do?' Fred asked, now curious.

'That day in Phnom Penh, George and I were sitting in the kitchen with the children of the maid. George was excited about a butterfly net he just got for his tenth birthday and was swinging it around as we were having bread and jam,' JJ said.

***

JJ and George were still at the table when the other two younger children sprang from their seats, ready to disappear into the garden. In her incomprehensible language, the maid held them back; she knelt in front of her children and whispered to them. Then she got up and with a shy smile, she shooed her children, JJ, and George outside. The children took JJ's hand and pulled him.

'Come see cricket,' they urged him.

JJ had been wanting to see the pet insects for a while. The children kept them well hidden, because the crickets were sacred to them and they were afraid someone would steal them.

'George, are you coming? They are finally showing us their crickets.'

'Non, I don't care about their crickets. I heard they let them fight each other.'

'Really? How can that be?' JJ tried to ask the children, but their French was not sufficient to understand or answer.

'*Vas-y*, go, if you want. I will go butterfly hunting and catch a beautiful one for you to draw.'

'Maman always warned me not to wander alone in the garden; there might be snakes, she said. Maybe I should stay here with you.'

'No, you go. I can stay here alone. If a snake comes, I will kill it with my magic wand and put it in the butterfly net,' George said as he picked up the wooden handle of his new butterfly net and swung it in the air.

JJ hesitated for a moment, then hurried to follow the children, who were waiting for him with bored expressions. Halfway over, he stopped and turned to look back. 'Be careful, George,' he said, waving. JJ did not know it was the last time he would see his cousin alive.

Much later that day, JJ returned home with a small bamboo toy the children had given him to play with. As he entered the living room, he first saw his Aunt Juliette crying at the table.

His mother bumped into a chair as she rushed toward him. 'Where have you been, JJ?' she asked roughly. 'We have been looking for you forever. Who gave you permission to leave the house?'

'I went to my friends' home.'

'Your friends? They are not your *friends*, you stupid boy,' his aunt shouted from the table. She turned to his mother and said, 'I told you that your boy was fine, and he had just left George alone in the garden. Just as selfish as his parents.'

JJ felt as if his limbs had been paralyzed and he wanted to ask what had happened, but his mother's stony expression stopped him. He then saw his father approach in a hurry, home unusually early that day.

'I came as soon as I heard. What happened?' his father asked, placing his hands on his sister's shaking shoulders.

'Juliette and I were looking for JJ, who was nowhere to be found, George was in the garden playing. We did not notice that after a while, George was missing too. He had gone to the ravine, and a snake had bitten him. When we found him, he was already unconscious.'

'Didn't you call the doctor, for heaven's sake?'

'It took us too long to find George and call the doctor. They brought him to the military hospital but… ' JJ's mother tried hard not to cry, 'the poison… the snake, they did not know what it was. They gave him something but…he… he died two hours ago.'

Stunned, JJ let the fragile bamboo toy fall on the floor and stepped on it as he ran to his room, where his father found him a little while later. JJ apologised between his sobs and tears for leaving George alone. His father commanded JJ to stay in his room for several days, and he could not attend George's funeral.

From that day, he barely left the house. The maid disappeared and so did her children, leaving JJ with no company for the rest of their stay in Phnom Penh. He barely saw his parents: his father was often on business trips and his mother seemed too busy. She stopped coming to see him in his room, where he spent most of his time, and she often left him alone for lunches as well.

'My aunt accused me of leaving George alone,' JJ now told Fred in their cabin. Sitting on the floor, he struggled to swallow his tears.

Fred, who was on his knees next to his friend, was forlorn hearing the desperation in JJ's voice, and he felt guilty for ripping George's portrait. He tried to reassure JJ and downplay his role in his cousin's accident.

'Come on, now,' Fred started. 'It is terrible, of course, but it was not really your fault. You didn't know about the snake.'

'I did. My mother told me there were snakes. I should have taken care of him,' JJ replied.

'Nobody expected you to do so, you were a child as well.'

'Oh yes, I told you. My aunt was right. And the icy stare of my mother… ' JJ squeezed his eyes to chase the image away. 'Do you understand, Fred? I killed my little cousin, my only friend. I killed him because I left him alone to go play with children who were not my friends.'

'Come on,' Fred said, 'you cannot say they were not your friends, they even gave you a toy, right?'

'They did not care about me,' JJ said, brushing the corner of his eye, where a tear was burning.

'Even if they didn't, who cares? You had Old Min,' Fred said, patting JJ's shoulder. 'And now you have me. I am more than your friend. We are sworn brothers, right?'

JJ breathed deeply to stop his tears, which were now tracing a line on his cheeks. He wiped his eyes with the back of his hands. 'Yes, you are right. You are my friend.'

'I'll go and find some glue. We can put the pieces together. It will be like a puzzle,' Fred said, and he rose and opened the cabin door with determination, leaving JJ with a grateful look.

It did not take long to piece the drawing together and after a short while, Fred became restless again.

'I have to go out! I cannot accept this injustice,' he said.

'You heard your brother. He even asked one crewman to make sure you would not leave,' JJ said. 'What if something happens?' Under his breath, he added, 'Like when I left George alone.'

Fred looked around for his luggage, then he took some bills from the interior pocket, like his brother earlier did. 'We can use money to convince him to let us leave,' Fred said with a big smile. 'I am sure he would not mind.'

'You want to bribe him?' JJ replied, his voice higher than usual. Bribery had been a part of daily life in Indochina, except, of course, it was not defined as such.

'It's an excellent investment, JJ. This time you must come with me. I won't accept a refusal.'

'I don't know. I don't think it is a good idea. Your brother will get mad.'

'My brother will never know; we will be back before the time is up. Just bring some money with you to have a couple of drinks and a real Hong Kong meal instead of the French version they serve on board.' He pushed his friend in front of the tiny porthole. 'Look! Look at the sky. It is so blue, so inviting. You stayed on the ship for almost a month. Don't you want to get out?' Fred asked, putting his arm on JJ's shoulder. They were now sitting on the lower berth.

'Actually, no. I feel no urge to leave the boat. I quite like observing the passengers boarding.'

'But observing those who live here is even more interesting. Think about all the beautiful sketches you can make.'

Fred could see that JJ was still not convinced. He moved to the middle of the cabin and stood in front of JJ with his legs apart, firmly rooted to the floor.

'JJ, you have to help me. You know I cannot speak English. If you don't come and I lose my way, I would not be able to come back on time and then… your friend will be in trouble.'

JJ sucked his breath in. 'Okay, okay, I will come. But just a couple of hours.'

Fred whooped and jumped with joy.

*** 

Outside, they found the sailor in charge on the deck. The young man accepted the money with eagerness and let them leave the ship with no trouble.

'That was easy,' Fred said, and he took a deep breath.

Once on firm ground, the two friends looked around and saw that the pier opened into a square where a double-decker bus was waiting for passengers to alight before moving a few metres forward to the terminus. The bus driver flipped the destination sign, then got out for a smoke.

With firm steps, Fred started walking along the seafront, but JJ stopped him.

'Wait, the ships all look the same here. We have to find out where we are. Let me ask.'

JJ approached the bus driver, who was idling with a cigarette between his fingers. JJ noticed the fingernails on his pinkies were much longer than those on his other fingers, a practice among many Asians JJ had met before. The driver's face had a sandy colour similar to natural leather, and his hair was thick and black. JJ crossed his fingers that he wouldn't need to test his meagre Chinese skills. The driver did not seem to speak much English, but he could tell JJ the name of the pier.

'Balake Piel,' the driver said.

JJ rushed back to Fred. 'We have a name. Blake Pier. Let's check which street we are in.'

'I am glad you take your guide job so seriously,' Fred said as he watched JJ look for a street sign.

'Connaught Road. Good.'

'Okay, lead the way. I will follow you,' Fred said with a quick bow.

'Well, I have a feeling that if we rely on you, we might end up missing the ship.'

'Never in my life. I don't want to become minced meat in the hands of my brother.'

Their laughter reverberated in the empty square as the pair vanished into an alley to find a main road. At the corner, they stopped to take in their surroundings.

The convulsive traffic took them both by surprise.

'Eh bien, I was wrong… I thought the sea was pretty full, but it is nothing compared to this,' Fred said.

'This is three times the chaos in Indochina,' JJ replied.

Cars and trucks were parked along the pavement. On the road, bicycles fought with red-and-green rickshaws, and cars had to share the road with trams and double-decker buses. The endless crowd of people was matched by the countless signs hanging from the buildings or glued to pillars. JJ noted the sheer number of characters on display could have filled a whole calligraphy book.

'Fred, if you keep turning your head like that, it will twist off your neck.'

'I know, my head is spinning. Do you see that man? He is wearing pyjamas right in the middle of the street!'

JJ looked at the man in loose trousers and jacket, whose fabric and pattern could indeed have fit in the pages of a *Decré* catalogue, in the nightwear section. Elderly ladies wore long black dresses that were tight on the body and had a slit on the side; some were in a shorter version, ending after the waist, paired with large trousers that stopped at the ankles. Cone hats were as widespread here as among the coolies JJ and Fred saw in the Saigon harbour. The two men's white faces and typical Western clothing were conspicuous amid the crowd, but people ignored them.

'How strange. Here nobody looks at us,' JJ said.

'Well, we are not running around in our PJs.'

'What I mean is that in Indochina, I always felt people staring at me. I had the impression of being constantly spied on or that I had something on my face.'

'Probably they did not like your big nose,' Fred said with a laugh.

'You are joking, but it is probably true. My friend Old Min told me that foreigners are called 'long nose' in China.'

'They are probably just envious. Your nose looks fine to me,' Fred said, 'but maybe you want to consider doing some sport, my chap. You look sickish after spending all that time on the ship.' He pushed his friend with his hand. 'You are as light as a feather.'

'At least I don't have trouble closing the buttons of my jacket, as you have,' JJ said, remembering the day Fred despaired for having gained a couple of kilos.

'Ah, so true.' Fred sighed while he patted his stomach. Then he grinned. 'I'm feeling hungry now. Shall we find something to eat?'

# Chapter 10

JJ and Fred turned into a market's side street overflowing with shoppers, vendors selling their wares, suppliers, and onlookers. Goods were kept in a myriad of straw baskets, giving the two friends the impression that the street was narrower than it really was. Some stalls had flat wooden planks on which their merchandise was displayed in strange combinations. Now and then, the two came upon open-air butcher blocks, where small pieces of meat were waiting to be bought. Larger cuts of pork and beef hung on hooks, for the delight of the flies and other insects.

JJ and Fred saw a woman take a screaming chicken from a cage; then, with a firm hand, she pulled its neck and chopped it with a heavy cleaver. Horrified and fascinated, they watched how the blood spilled from the open neck while the headless bird ran around, convulsions shaking its body. The laughter of a few waiting customers brought JJ and Fred back to reality, and exchanging a look, they hurried away from the scene.

'After that, I think I will stop eating chicken,' Fred said.

'Or meat altogether,' JJ replied.

'Right. Let's get out of here, before I lose any interest in food.'

The adjacent street was by no means less crowded. This time, the most disparate activities filled the entire lane. JJ and Fred passed a woman having her hair styled outside while her friends waited for her, giggling; on their right, men were having their beards trimmed. A group of elderly men were close by, all squatting around a gameboard. The banging of the cobbler drowned the onlookers' commentary of the game. There was even an outdoor dentist who busied himself with a patient's teeth using rudimentary tools.

'I am surprised one is not shouting,' Fred said, showing the dentist's chair and the poor chap sitting on it.

'You are right. It looks like life is happening outside, in the open air and in front of everybody. No privacy whatsoever,' JJ said. 'I don't think I want to be on display while somebody cleans my ears with a cotton swab.' He pointed to a couple occupied thusly a few metres away. 'I'll clean my ears myself,' he added.

'Okay, let's stop here. I don't want to picture you cleaning your ears,' Fred said. A smile flashed on his face. 'That restaurant there looks decent.'

JJ looked at the restaurant across the street. 'I thought you didn't want to eat chicken anymore.' The restaurant had two large windowpanes, in one of them were five cooked geese hanging from hooks.

'Those aren't chicken. And they still have their heads,' Fred replied, and he went inside.

They sat on wooden stools at one of the round tables with no tablecloth. Fred took a chopstick from the bamboo cutlery holder, examined it, and put it back, rubbing his fingers together afterwards as if to get rid of the dust. He sniffed around without making a noise. 'At least here it smells like food. Is there a menu?'

'What do you want a menu for? We can't read anything anyway,' JJ said, but he still looked around to find one. He noticed strips of paper hanging on the wall.

'I think the menu is written on those banners. I'm afraid I can't really understand much. Old Min never taught me the character for chicken… ' JJ said.

'You are then lucky you have me, pal,' Fred said. He got up and walked around the restaurant, his hands deep in his pockets. A fat waiter came up to him and, with confidence, Fred ordered a few dishes, pointing to the appetising ones he saw on the other tables.

'Well, you can be resourceful,' JJ said, with an admiring smile.

'When we are talking food, I can find my way,' Fred said.

Next to them, two customers were eating chicken and spitting the bones out directly on the table; JJ and Fred stifled their laughter, thinking that such behaviour back home would have banned them from family dinners for a while. After the customers left, a waiter collected the bones with a cloth that looked like it had not been cleaned all day, spreading the grease all over the table. JJ and Fred looked at each other, then down at their table. A split second later, they lifted their elbows and hands from the surface, a grimace on their faces. From another table in a corner, a customer cleared his throat and spit into a spittoon. Unable to control themselves anymore, JJ and Fred exploded into belly laughs.

'That was the most thorough throat-clearing I've ever heard,' Fred said.

'Yes,' JJ agreed, covering his mouth with his hand to hide his laughter. 'He might have expelled his lungs.'

Fred guffawed even louder.

JJ was actually accustomed to this habit, as Old Min had often done the same. The first time JJ heard Old Min clearing his throat, JJ thought his teacher was feeling sick and wanted to throw up. The unease JJ felt when he heard the sound was still there, but the spitting did not surprise him anymore.

Finally, their dishes came: Fred managed to order chicken (how the hell would they eat that, with no knives and forks?), vegetables, and a soup with noodles. JJ's friendship with Old Min came in handy once again as he recalled how he was taught how to use chopsticks. Now JJ could show Fred how to hold them.

'Look, you take one chopstick and rest the top end at the base of the thumb and the middle part on your ring finger, like this, you see? Now, take the second one and hold it between your thumb and index finger, resting it on your middle finger. Look, one chopstick remains steady in the hand, while the other one can move easily.'

The other customers watched as Fred carefully held his chopsticks and tried to pick up a piece of chicken. They giggled more or less overtly, and when Fred succeeded, there was even a small round of applause. The waiter gave Fred a thumbs-up from the other side of the restaurant, where he was serving new patrons.

Spitting the chicken bones onto the table was unthinkable for them, so JJ and Fred used their hands to take the bones from their mouths. At first, they placed them on the plate of vegetables. Soon, however, there were too many bones, and they resigned to placing them on the table with a sigh.

And once their noodle soup had cooled enough, they enjoyed imitating the other customers: they each placed one end of a noodle in the mouth, then sucked it in noisily. With the soup, they slurped it up from a spoon like small children, unaware of the turn their friendship would take.

\*\*\*

After JJ and Fred left the restaurant and had walked around for some time, they came to a junction that was empty of shops but still full of pedestrians.

'What is all the fuss here?' Fred said while they approached a low white building from which people were coming in and out.

JJ read the nearby sign aloud. 'Peak Tram. Right, that's Victoria Peak the banker talked about. Shall we go up, Fred?'

They bought their tickets and boarded the tram, which rapidly filled up with locals and foreigners enjoying a Sunday outing. Behind JJ and Fred, the voices of a group of four or five rose above the cheerful chatter, and among the snippets of laughter, Fred heard French words spoken. He turned to look at the group: three Western men and two Asian women, all dressed casually in Western clothes.

Once the tram arrived at its upper terminal, the doors opened, and Fred and JJ were pushed out of the carriage by the stream of passengers. In a few minutes, they reached the terrace of the highest viewpoint.

'Can you see our ship?'

'No, I can't. There are too many,' JJ replied.

Beyond Victoria Harbour, they saw the seafront on the other side, where ferries were docking at or departing from several piers. In the background, there was a small range of mountains. While they enjoyed the view, the same group who was giggling in the tram earlier came closer, giving Fred the chance to strike up a conversation.

Fred learned that apart from one man, they were all colleagues from a local car dealer, Hua Nan Motors, which sold American and French cars to affluent

Hongkongese and foreigners. The two male colleagues were sharing a flat and a car.

'Our boss lent the car to us, as a way to advertise it. We are some of the most sought-after men in the company thanks to the car,' one of them said, looking at their pretty Asian colleagues.

'We're going to Aberdeen. Why don't you join?' he said to Fred and JJ. 'A floating restaurant opened a couple of years ago. You can get the best fish ever there. We have two cars, and you can ride with Roger.' He pointed at the older man next to him. 'He's Dutch and works for a Dutch trading company.'

JJ looked at his watch, frowning. 'We actually ate a short while ago.'

'You can still join us. What are you up to, otherwise?' Roger asked.

'We need to be back at the ship by eight pm,' JJ said.

'Aberdeen is just on the other side of the hill. By car, we won't need much time. I can drive you back to the harbour,' Roger said.

Fred looked at his friend. 'Come on, JJ, we still have plenty of time. It's not even three pm. It sounds much more fun than being on our own. They know better where to go.'

Seeing Fred's eagerness to go with the group, JJ relented. 'Do you know how long it takes from there to the harbour?' he asked Roger.

'About forty minutes, one hour at most if we find an idiot in front of us who is afraid of driving,' Roger said.

JJ looked at his watch again. 'Can you take us back at six?'

'Mou man tai. No problem,' Roger said.

'Watch out, guys. You will get a crash course in Cantonese cursing if Roger meets a poor driver,' one of the French men joked, laughing.

# Chapter 11

JJ and Fred discovered Aberdeen was a fishing village. One could barely see the water of the bay as sampans of all sizes jostled for space, expanding Hong Kong's living options beyond the waterfront. The different shades of brown of the boats, and the white and occasional red of their sails created a colourful picture that JJ was already busy drawing in his mind. Just as it was in the market, lives were lived outside for all to see: dirty children played around the shore, men were busy cleaning fish or repairing their nets, women were cooking at the rear of the sampans, throwing food waste into the water.

The group of seven crossed a wooden plank over the water to enter the imposing floating restaurant. Inside, the lavish decorations in white, red, and gold gave the three-storey construction an opulent and majestic air; a cacophony of voices and rattling tableware filled the huge dining hall, which accommodated well over a hundred guests. The spacious hall was not divided and the largest round tables could seat up to twenty diners each. Waiters in uniforms inspired by traditional clothing were running from one side to the other, holding large trays full of food or empty dishes. JJ and Fred felt like they had stepped into another world.

They sat at one of the smaller round tables, allowing them to talk without shouting too loudly. Not sharing the same language, the group conversed in a mix of English and French. This time, JJ did not hide his knowledge of English and often translated for Fred.

Roger turned towards JJ. 'Are you also fluent in Chinese?'

JJ's face flushed, and he said that indeed he could speak a little.

The girls' expressions brightened in delight and they started speaking quickly in their sing-song voices, 'Nei sik gong zungman ah? Nei giu med ye meng? Nei hei bin dou yen ah?' Then they burst into laughter, their black pupils disappearing behind the squeezed eyelids of their small eyes. JJ's lost expression made the girls giggle even more.

'These naughty girls… They are speaking Cantonese, not the Chinese a foreigner would study,' Roger said.

'Right, I heard Cantonese was not the same, but I did not realise that the differences would be so striking,' JJ said.

'Oh, yes.'

'How is life in Hong Kong?'

'Since the communists are in power in China, Hong Kong imported a sizeable chunk of triad members, who thought they would have free wheel here. Which they basically have, as long as they play the game with Her Highness's police,' Roger said.

'What do you mean?' JJ asked. 'Aren't the police supposed to respect and enforce the law?'

'In your dreams, maybe. Or in Europe. But here, there is one only rule: get rich. And the higher you are in the police, the higher your chances of striking a convenient deal that will lead to even higher positions and more money. But you should know… life in the French colonies is not so different. The strongest rules and imposes on others,' Roger said, cracking his knuckles.

The conversation continued on a lighter note, and JJ noticed how the two girls were clearly at the centre of attention of the small group; Fred, who could only indirectly take part in the discussions, was content to stare at them with an ecstatic smile. He whispered to JJ that he was not sure whether he liked their shiny black hair more or their lips.

Fred was fascinated by their curious gesture with their hands when they laughed. He wondered whether they covered their mouths because they did not want to be loud or because they had rotten teeth.

Roger also showed a mild interest in one of the girls, but he was not willing to make the effort to compete with the younger fellows for her attention. Thus he made smaller gestures, such as stopping the lazy Susan in the right spot so she could take from her favourite dish. He once chose a nice, juicy piece of shrimp and put it straight into her bowl, getting as a thank a tiny nod from the lovely young woman.

The two girls did not seem to have any favourites among their admirers, sharing equally their attention and their laughter, and enjoying the singular company of the foreigners. JJ wondered whether their friendliness was real or had hidden motives, as the maid's children had.

The lunch lasted longer than planned, and when JJ looked at his watch, he jumped up from his chair. 'It's already past six! We need to make our way back to the ship. Roger, could you take us back now?'

'Sure, of course. I am glad to,' Roger said.

Moments later, Roger, JJ, and Fred had said their goodbyes to the rest of the group and were walking towards Roger´s car. As they approached, a fisherman carrying a pole on his shoulder, from which two baskets were hanging, bumped into Roger, and the car keys he had in his hand fell to the ground. As Roger bent to pick them up, JJ and Fred heard him swearing under his breath, and then hold his back.

Roger unlocked the driver's door but made no move to open it, holding himself steady with his hand on the car roof, eyes closed.

'Are you all right?' JJ asked.

Roger inhaled deeply and said, 'No, my back... I guess I made a wrong movement while bending. Can you drive, JJ?'

JJ was taken aback and hesitated. 'Well, I do have a driving licence, but I never drove on the right side. Besides, I am not sure I am comfortable driving your car.'

'Well, my boy, I'm afraid I'm at the moment in no position to drive, and if you want to reach the harbour in time, you must drive, at least until we reach the city. By then my back should be better and I can take over,' Roger said, walking towards JJ and handing him the keys.

Fred looked surprised, as he did not understand the exchange between Roger and JJ.

'Zut, that's not fair you get to drive,' Fred said.

'Do you have a driving licence?' JJ asked as he stood at the driver's door.

Roger guessed what the two were saying and cut Fred off.

'No, JJ, you drive. And open the damned door, I need to sit down.'

JJ hurried to get in the car and leaned over to unlock the front passenger door to let Roger in, then he did the same with the back door for Fred. JJ started the engine carefully and, following Roger's directions, took a winding road which lead towards the harbour.

The car hugged the hilly landscape, while the sea below played hide and seek at each turn. The boats dotted the water like dark shadows.

'How long are you two staying in China?' Roger asked, glancing briefly at JJ sitting next to him.

'Fred and his brother are part of a trade delegation. They are staying about two weeks. I am not sure how long I will stay,' JJ replied, thinking about his mission in Hangzhou.

'What are your plans afterwards? Planning to go back to France? By sea again?'

'Probably, yes.'

'I see. You will come back to Hong Kong then,' Roger said. 'We should keep in touch, lad, you know… ' He reached into the glove compartment, took out a business card, and passed it to JJ while they stopped at a red light.

'Roger Whittle, Holland China Trading Company,' JJ read aloud. 'What do you do there, Roger?'

'Oh, I work as an employee. I do this and that. It depends on what I am asked to look for. I have my regular suppliers, for example, for ceramics. They are cheap in Asia and sell well in Europe.'

*'This and that.' I bet it is not the complete story*, thought JJ. *You look like that officer who sold army supplies to the expat families. Well, none of my business. I doubt I will meet you again.* He put the card in his pocket as the light turned green.

As JJ was taking a turn, he suddenly saw a car standing motionless a few metres away, causing JJ to swerve quickly and vigorously apply the brakes. Despite JJ's efforts, the car slid forwards and hit the vehicle in front; the impact was powerful enough that Roger and JJ hit the windshield with their foreheads, while Fred somehow protected his head and was not hurt.

Outside, they saw a car lying on its side and another looking severely damaged. Two people were sitting in shock next to the road, while a third one was slumped over the steering wheel of one car, seemingly dead. Roger's car had hit the third car, whose driver had got out to give a hand.

'You're hurt. You're hurt. You are bleeding,' Fred shouted, seeing a rivulet of blood flowing from JJ's forehead.

JJ felt numb and speechless, while Roger, who only suffered a slight nick in the forehead, had recovered quickly. 'Let's get out. We risk being hit by a driver behind us,' he said, moving slowly to manage his back pain.

The owner of the third car approached Roger frantically, but Roger was busy at trying to stop any more cars from hitting the pile-up. JJ and Fred sat at the edge of the road, their faces white and their bodies shaking. JJ held a handkerchief to his forehead to stop the blood while Fred tried to see how serious the injury was.

'The blood has stopped, and the wound seems to be superficial. How do you feel?' Fred asked JJ.

'I'm fine, I'm fine. But how are we going to get back to the ship now? The road is blocked,' JJ said.

'Merde,' Fred cursed, biting his lip.

Roger came back to check the damage to his car, and was followed by the driver he had hit who kept shouting in Cantonese. Roger silenced him with a thick wad of banknotes.

By now, traffic in both directions had stalled, making any rescue more difficult.

'Roger, I am so sorry,' JJ said, getting on his feet.

'You drove fine. It could have happened to me as well. Are you okay?' Roger asked, noticing his wound.

'I'm okay, but our ship is leaving soon. What are we going to do?' JJ asked.

Roger looked around, his hands on his hips. 'The road will be blocked for some time, for sure. When the next bus comes along, it will get even worse.' He passed his hand through his hair, and only then noticed the slight cut on his forehead, still half-wet with blood. He dismissed it with a grunt, then walked past the damaged cars, all the way to a Ford Anglia, which had been driving in the opposite direction before being stalled. There were no cars behind the Anglia.

From a distance, JJ and Fred saw Roger speaking to the driver and showing him a sum of money from his wallet. He returned and handed the money to them.

'The man over there has agreed to turn around and take you to the port with this money,' Roger said. 'You have my card. If something goes wrong, call me.'

The two grateful young men took the money and hurried towards the car, getting in quickly after a nod from the Chinese driver. The driver, who looked twice their age, turned the vehicle into the other lane and they were off.

During the ride, JJ and Fred gripped the seats in front of them while their hair stood up on end. The windows were down, and the wind whipped at their faces as the car careened downhill. When they finally entered the urban streets, the two friends relaxed a little. The car had now slowed to a crawl.

'Oh là là, are we driving with Dr Jekyll and Mr Hyde?' Fred said a few moments later.

'Well, better a little slower to avoid another accident,' JJ said.

'Oui, but if we keep moving so slowly, we are really going to miss the ship.'

'We should not be far from the harbour. I think the Peak Tram station is over there. You see the queue? By car, it won't take long to reach Blake Pier,' JJ said, showing a point in the distance.

'I cannot see anything. The buildings are so close to each other.'

The Ford Anglia kept moving in slow motion next to a crowded double-decker tram, carrying its passengers home from their Sunday excursions.

Red light, stop. Green. The car moved forward two metres. Red light, stop. Green.

JJ looked at his watch. 'Kuài, kuài! Hurry, hurry!' JJ pressed the driver, who just gave him a look through the rear-view mirror without changing the speed.

JJ and Fred anxiously searched for any sign of the harbour.

'My stomach hurts,' JJ said.

Finally, a right turn offered a wider view, and the harbour and Kowloon appeared. Several ships could be spotted near the dock. The car travelled alongside the harbour, passing slowly in front of ferries and smaller boats, then stopped at Blake Pier. JJ and Fred paid the driver and got out of the car.

The pier was empty.

'It's… gone.' Fred was the first to speak.

JJ kept looking at the sea and then around them. 'This is the right pier.'

'The ship is gone! But it must be a mistake.'

'There is no mistake. The ship left without us. On est dans la merde.'

'It cannot be,' Fred said, and shook his head. 'It is a mistake. The ship will come back. We must wait for it. Come on, let's sit over there.' It was the same attitude he had when he refused to acknowledge he had lost a chess game.

*I am afraid this is not a chess game, and we lost more than a king,* JJ thought. But he indulged his friend for now.

'Maybe you are right. Let's wait for a while,' he said to Fred.

# Chapter 12

The two friends sat on the raised sidewalk for over an hour, scanning the ships coming and going in the harbour. Fred was still in a chatty mood, as if he were just waiting for his bus to arrive. JJ listened to him in silence, unable to move. When an unknown ship pulled in to dock at Blake Pier, JJ saw his friend's bright expression finally change to worry. Still, he was unwilling to give up.

'Maybe our ship docked somewhere else. We should have a look,' Fred said, getting up.

'No,' JJ replied, 'ships never come back if a passenger fails to board.' He told Fred that on one of two long voyages he took with his parents, a missionary had gone ashore in Colombo but had returned too late to board. A young JJ had stood among a crowd of passengers, looking upset as they watched the priest on the dock, waving his arms and shouting at the top of his lungs. The captain had explained that the ship was too big to turn around and that reversing course in the open sea and sailing back would take too long.

Fred frowned. 'Why didn't you say that before, instead of letting us wait here for nothing?'

JJ's mouth opened to answer, but before he could, Fred got up and started walking along the pier, putting his hands in his trouser pockets.

'Wait, where are you going?' JJ asked, following him.

'I don't know, but I think you were mean to let me believe that the ship was coming back.'

JJ's face scrunched up. 'I… I didn't say that. I told you that it wasn't a mistake, but you didn't want to hear it.'

'So what? You should have insisted instead of letting me wait,' Fred said.

'Sorry,' JJ said, the corners of his mouth twitching nervously. He lowered his head. 'I really thought… '

'Whatever,' Fred said dryly, 'that's fine. What are we going to do now? We just have a few dollars left.' His hands were still in his pocket as he challenged JJ to come up with a suitable answer.

'I guess the only option is to contact our families to send us some money,' JJ said.

'I don't think that's a good idea. I don't want my mother to worry. My brother will be furious enough and I don't need additional problems.'

'What other options do we have, Fred? With barely any cash… '

'I know what we can do,' Fred said.

The silence was thick and longer than normal as JJ looked at Fred with anticipation.

'We have Roger's card. Let's call him. He could lend us some money.'

Another long pause, then JJ licked his dry lips and said, 'I am not sure that's a good idea. The guy is not completely straight.'

'Why do you say that? He looks like a nice chap to me. He even paid for our ride.'

JJ felt Fred's eyes on him and his ears got hot.

'Well, if you don't want to, I will call him. Just give me his card,' Fred said, stretching his hand towards JJ.

JJ swallowed while he found the card. 'You're right. We need a place to stay tonight, at least. There, let's use that payphone.'

With sweaty hands, JJ dialled the number and waited. The phone rang several times with no answer.

95

'He might still be blocked on the road. We better try later again.'

'What do we do now?' Fred said.

'I saw a church nearby. Let's go there and see if it is still open. At least we need no money to wait there.'

\*\*\*

JJ appraised the small but exquisite style of the Cathedral of the Immaculate Conception, its ceiling reaching high into the sky and its floor chequered. Inside it was pleasantly cool and an enjoyable break from the sticky humidity they had felt the whole day. It was almost empty, except for a few people praying, and no priest was in sight.

They sat on a bench and JJ stared into nothing ahead, lost in his thoughts. He was as far as ever from keeping his promise to Old Min. The urn and the addresses he needed were in his luggage, on the ship. He had no way to contact anybody and was afraid to miss his appointment with Old Min's daughter. He needed to reach Shanghai and get his luggage as soon as possible. Something told him that Roger was a dubious character, but he admitted he liked even less the option of calling his parents. He had not heard from them nor given them news of his travels since he left Paris.

'Do you often go to church?' Fred asked.

'We used to go before. It was a must while we stayed in Phnom Penh,' JJ said. 'It was the social event of the week. My mother and my aunt used to wear their nicest clothes, and there were all these silly girls and young army officials, laughing at each other.'

'Only the French attended the church?'

'No, of course not. Many locals went too, but their manners were so French, you would forget that they were born there.'

'They were also Christian?'

'Maybe, I don't know. But afterwards they were always happy to share a drink in good company. I guess it was also a place where they discussed business. So, not sure how much they believed in God.'

'Do you believe in God?'

'I guess not really, after all.'

'Oh, me neither. Then we cannot pray for help.' Fred laughed, but JJ did not join him. 'Come on, crack at least a smile.'

'If I miss my meeting with Old Min's daughter, I might not reach her otherwise. She had arranged for special permission to meet me. I must keep my promise.'

\*\*\*

In the evening, Fred became increasingly alarmed when he realised Roger was not coming to rescue them, that the night would swallow them and force them to sleep on the streets.

The night breeze kept JJ and Fred keenly aware of their place of rest: a makeshift bed on a tiny green parcel outside, close to the church. In the morning, the wind was still blowing, the misty air penetrating deep into their bones.

Fred's fear was gone, and in its place was regret.

'I'm cold and hungry,' he grumbled.

'I know, you told me already,' JJ said, nodding as a parent would when a child asks for something incessantly.

'Why did we leave the ship? That was so stupid.'

'Look, the sunrise. The weather will get warm soon. Let's go to the harbour again. Maybe we can find something to eat there.'

At five o'clock the pier was already buzzing: coolies were transporting goods up and down the docked ships and tiny shops were preparing to open their doors. At a string of tables and stools occupying the free space between two warehouses, a few workers were eating white soup with something swimming in it; others held fried pastries they bit into after dipping it in a dark sauce. Neither option looked very inspiring to the two friends, but the emptiness of their stomachs pushed them to sit with the workers and order food. The waiter set down two bowls of soup noodles, which turned out to be mercifully cheap and filling.

Fred concentrated on his food, chewing longer than usual before swallowing with a grimace.

JJ also ate in silence, looking around.

The activity at the port was picking up by the minute, with new coolies joining those already there; farther along, more warehouses were opening their doors as small trucks and wooden carts stopped in front of them to load the goods for the shops in town. Coolies loaded long rolls of fabric onto the carts, nearly all with typical Chinese patterns, some dark, some in bright colours. JJ admired the ravishing designs of the material, depicting with high precision flowers and birds, animals and pagodas, and he wondered how a dress from such a fabric would look on a woman. It was obviously expensive, but the coolies did not care. With their filthy and greasy hands, they put them in a cart not much cleaner than the pavement.

He turned and looked at Fred. They needed to reach Roger as soon as possible. They walked back to the phone box and tried again. This time Roger picked up.

'Hello?'

JJ let out a little cry. 'Hello, Roger! So sorry to wake you up. We need your help. We missed the ship,' JJ said in one breath.

'Who is speaking? What ship? Why the ship?'

'It's Jean-Jacques speaking. We met yesterday, remember? You gave us your card… ' JJ hesitated. 'We were supposed to get the ship to go to Shanghai, but there was a car accident and we were too late.' JJ hoped the amount of information was at this point sufficient. He was sure Roger had spent the night drinking.

'Ah, yes, of course. Now I remember. Sure. You missed the ship. I see,' Roger said. 'Where are you now?'

'We are close to the harbour. We did not know where to go.'

They talked back and forth until Roger had a clear idea of their location.

'Go to the church again. I will come and pick you up from the front,' he said.

The two friends reached the church again and waited for Roger. They killed time by mimicking the locals they saw squatting, their knees spread open and heels on the ground. Their legs, though, were not agile enough to enable them to squat without lifting their heels, thus they kept falling on their buttocks and laughing at each other's clumsiness. When Roger arrived, he looked at the scene and a veil of melancholy fell over his face. He called out to JJ and Fred.

While Roger drove back to his flat, they told him about missing the boat, spending the night outside, and eating unfamiliar food. Roger seemed to be only half listening, concentrating on the road to avoid hitting anything or anyone. He lived rather outside the central area of the island; his flat was on the second floor of a modest but well-kept building, with a narrow staircase illuminated by a single light bulb on each floor, where two doors faced each other. The lodging was quite small, with one bedroom large enough for only a double bed and a wardrobe; the living room had a worn-out couch, a table, and a few chairs; the kitchen was practically non-existent, confined to a corner between the two rooms.

Fred smiled. 'Ah, nice to be in a flat.' He sniffed at his shirt. 'My clothes smell like fish and fried food.'

JJ teased him a little, but he then asked Roger if it was possible to take a bath.

'No, you can't. Water has been rationed for a while and we cannot waste it with baths or showers; if you want, I collected some water in a basin and you can use it for a quick wash, but mind you, don't spill it or throw it away afterwards. I've already used it twice, so don't expect clean water either,' Roger explained.

JJ saw Fred's expression change when he translated his answer.

'Why is the water rationed?' JJ asked.

'Hong Kong simply does not have enough water for the entire population,' Roger replied. 'The government is dealing with China to get some from them, but there are strong political pressures against this deal.'

He went to the kitchenette to prepare coffee, which he put on the table with a tin of biscuits. He noticed the young men looking at the coffee with suspicion.

'Why are you looking like that? You think I prepared the coffee with the same water I washed myself with?' His booming laugh could have been heard in the hallway. 'So, you missed the boat. Don't worry, there are regular trips to Shanghai.'

'Well, we don't have money to buy tickets.'

'I can lend you the money. As long as you have your documents, there is no problem. Not sure about the schedule, but you can stay with me in the meantime. You'll have to share the couch, though,' he said, 'and use the recycled water.'

JJ slapped his head, only now recalling something important. 'Our passports!'

# Chapter 13

JJ rubbed his head, as if this could make the problem of their forgotten passports disappear.

'What? You left your passports on the ship?' Roger said. 'This is shit. How brainless... What were you thinking? That you were in France? Now, you listen. You always keep your documents with you, especially if you are going to China. I can lend you the money, but if you have no documents, they won't sell you a ticket, nor you can cross the border without identification. You must go to the French Commission and request new documents; this is the only alternative.'

'The French Commission? I did not think about this. Can they also help if you have no money?' JJ asked, with a hopeful look.

'I think they have options,' Roger said.

JJ translated to Fred but Fred was all but eager about the idea.

'No, no, we cannot go there. They will want some kind of proof of my identity. They will ask my mother. I told you she is unwell, and I cannot do that,' Fred said.

'But Fred, Roger is right. Without documents, we cannot go anywhere.'

Fred jumped from the worn out couch and paced about, repeating that it was not possible.

JJ explained to Roger the reason Fred did not want to go to the French Commission.

'Well, you discuss this while I make some more coffee.' Roger got up and left the two friends to continue their fervid conversation.

As Roger put another pot of coffee on the side table, JJ told him he could not persuade Fred. 'He is so stubborn, he said he would rather try to sneak on a ship and jump out once it reaches Shanghai.'

Roger looked hard at Fred. 'Ask him why,' he said.

'I told you why. His mother.'

'No, ask him why,' Roger said again. He looked straight into Fred's eyes and repeated 'why', sure that Fred would understand the word.

Under Roger's scrutiny, Fred repeated his story about his mother with much less assurance.

'Boy, if you don't tell us the reason you don't want to go to the French Commission, I don't think I can help you. I won't give my money to a liar. You can stay here today to figure out what you want to do, but tomorrow I want you out of here,' Roger said with his hands on his hips as if getting ready for a fight.

JJ startled.

Fred stopped passing one hand through his hair and took his head in both hands. He sat down again and muttered to the floor, 'They won't give it to me.'

'Why? Why would they not give you a new passport?' Roger asked.

'I am not twenty-one. I falsified a document to get the passport and bribed an employee at the city hall.' Fred looked around the room, arms on his knees, defeated.

JJ sat back in alarm, while Roger took in this information with interest.

Roger's voice was firm. 'Okay, we need to think of something else, then. I might have an idea, but this would entail some risks. But what about you, JJ? Are you going to the French Commission?'

'I think it is the best option,' JJ said. He was, though, now uncertain as he wondered what his friend was going to do. Roger's mention of risks made JJ uncomfortable.

'What do you have in mind for Fred? How can you help him?'

'I have to leave for work now and cannot stay longer. We can discuss it tonight at dinner. I'll pick you up at six pm. Here is a set of keys for the flat.' He also took some money from his wallet and gave it to them. 'Take this, go out, buy yourself some food. You can find Western goods in most supermarkets.'

He left the flat, leaving JJ and Fred to wonder how they could reach China without passports.

\*\*\*

Roger was idling in his office; in the ashtray on his desk was a half-smoked cigarette, which he left there as he became absorbed in his newspaper. He adjusted now and then the distance between him and the paper, squinting each time he turned a page. When he came to the last page, he sighed. He noticed his forgotten cigarette, took it and lighted it again. His fingers, which slightly trembled while he read the paper, were now steady and clasped around the cigarette. With one hand, he took a sip of his half-cold green tea as he looked at the clock. He was waiting for his colleagues to leave for lunch so he could be alone in the office. His wait did not last long, and he finally grabbed the phone to call his business partner, Cai Jun, in Guangzhou.

'Lao Cai, it's me, Roger.' He crushed his cigarette butt in the ashtray.

'What news?'

'I found the solution to our problems. It's the best solution to sell the helmet without implicating you directly,' Roger said and he explained his plan to Cai Jun.

'Maybe work okay,' Cai Jun said in broken English.

'They look like students. Nobody will touch them. I

am sure one will take the bait, but I need to work on his friend.'

'Can one go?'

'No, this man alone is not reliable and will make a mess. We need them both. I will think of something to convince him.'

Roger heard steps approaching his office. 'Okay, I cannot talk now. Call me at home later and we can make a plan.' He hung up and brought a hand to his chest, its heart pounding heavily in his chest.

***

Lying on the couch, JJ and Fred sipped their cans of soda and snacked on crisps they had bought from the supermarket.

'I know, it was so stupid what I did. But I so wanted to go with my brother. Spend time with him, you know… He has been a sort of hero to me as a child. At home they were always talking about him, whether it was at the grocery store or at the barber, or the local café, they all knew Marcel as a legend. I lied to him about my age, and he never knew. You see, he was already in the Legion when I was born. He would not have taken me if he knew that I was not of age yet,' Fred told his friend.

'But what about your parents? They know when you were born.'

'Yes, but my mother has been so busy with my father since his stroke, and she did not really know which documents we needed to go to China. She has never had a passport herself in her life.' It had been so easy, and he never expected to get into trouble for a little lie.

'What a mess,' JJ said.

'No, it is not a mess. It's just a hiccup. Roger will find a solution. He's like my brother, a tough guy. Maybe he will help me get on a ship and once we get to Shanghai, I sneak out,' Fred said, his words half drowned out by the crunching of the crisps.

'Aha, and how are you going to do that? Jump into the water and swim?'

Fred shrugged. The idea was not inviting. 'Not really. I don't think Roger has that in mind, anyway. I bet he has contacts to get a fake passport.'

'I would not be surprised. I have a feeling that of all the options, a fake passport could be the least bad,' JJ said, wiping his greasy hand on a towel he found in the kitchenette.

'Do you think so?' Fred said, his eyes bright. He liked the idea. 'As long as I don't have to swim, I am in!'

'It will probably cost you a fortune,' JJ said.

Fred's face darkened again. He always thought his parents were stingy, but once his brother came back, the stinginess reached another dimension, and meaning.

'Yes, I guess your brother won't be happy about the lie and the money, but in the end, you reached your goal of travelling with him. So, cheer up.'

Fred grunted. 'You joke, but I bet I can get a fake passport before you get yours from the French Commission. So, who will make it on time to Shanghai?' Fred said, without realising the bomb he had exploded in JJ's head.

JJ realised a new passport would not ensure he could keep his promise.

# Chapter 14

That night Roger took them to dinner at the Parisian Grill in Queen's Road. The restaurant was famous with the English crowd and with newly arrived foreigners who deemed their palate too fine for Asian food. It was, though, snubbed by most French people, who scorned its cooking as not authentic enough.

They had to go up a staircase to reach the main hall; from the unassuming street entrance they expected a small and quiet place, but the hall was surprisingly large and crowded.

'Are all restaurants so big here in Hong Kong, and so busy? It looks like people here are spending all their time eating,' JJ said.

'Here there are no weekends. Most people eat out because flats are too small to cook in, or too crowded with people. Many seek some space by going out. Those who can afford it come to fancy restaurants; those who have less money have a wide choice of street stalls everywhere in the city,' Roger explained, while they sat at a round table with a white tablecloth. The lights were dim; each table had its own chandelier around which the smoke of cigarettes would draw coloured shapes. Easy chairs were elegant but uncomfortable. In the impeccable setting, the restaurant was loud and vibrant, with a wide range of customers, including Westerners, Asians, Indians, and black people, each table apparently speaking a different language. The menu was not sophisticated, but it offered some comfort dishes. JJ ordered an onion soup, Fred and Roger steak with rice, and they agreed to share a bottle of red wine.

Fred sat relaxed and followed the conversation between Roger and JJ with his eyes.

'JJ, now that we know that Fred is still a minor, I guess you have the role of the big brother here, haven't you?' Roger asked, pouring the first glass of wine.

'Well, if I have, then maybe I should say that Fred is not allowed to drink wine yet.' JJ translated the exchange to Fred, who stretched out his arm to give his friend a fake punch. JJ widened his grin and laughed, showing his gums.

'I drank all the time on the ship. You will not forbid me anything now,' Fred said.

A sideways glance at Roger took the steam out of JJ and Fred's playful exchange and they regained their posture.

'So, Fred. This is what I can do for you. I can arrange to have you crossing the bay north of Hong Kong towards Bao' An County, where I have a friend who can help us. Once you are in China, my friend can get you a ticket to Shanghai. I warn you that the trip is long and not comfortable. The train is not direct, and you will have to stop in Changsha and get another train. You will still need help there to buy the ticket, and it is not sure that you will get one for the same day. Through my friend, I could get somebody to help you there too.'

Fred listened to JJ and as soon as he grasped the plan, he started in his seat. 'Yes, great idea. I told you he was like my brother, didn't I,' Fred said, and he flashed Roger a smile and nodded to show his agreement.

Roger was though looking straight into JJ's eyes instead of paying attention to Fred, as JJ gulped down some of the dry red wine.

'JJ, I know you have the option to get a passport, but are you sure you want to leave your friend alone?' Roger asked.

JJ stopped drinking and slowly lowered his glass to the table. 'What are the risks?'

Fred listened to JJ and Roger, but this time JJ did not offer any translation.

'Well, you are crossing the border illegally, thus there are some risks. If the Hong Kong police get you, they will simply question you and send you back home. If the Chinese police get you, it depends very much on whether they will think you are a spy or a fool,' Roger said, without mentioning that speaking any Chinese might make them more suspicious if they were caught. He said he did not expect major problems with the Hong Kong border guards, as they were more concerned about not letting people into Hong Kong than vice versa. Minor smuggling at the border, though officially not tolerated, was nonetheless widespread. The guards who turned a blind eye to it were lining their pockets quite well. They usually let people cross the border to China, provided they were as discreet as possible, but made sure to catch any living soul crossing in the inverse direction.

'When and how would this happen? Who are your friends? How can we communicate with them?' JJ asked.

'People I met through work; my friend can speak enough English. I would need to contact him to set a date, so it might still take a few days. How long is Fred's brother staying in Shanghai, you said?'

'Approximately two weeks.'

'We have to make sure you get there before your brother leaves, so you can get your passport,' he said. 'We should have sufficient time. The safest bet is to use a junk to get to the other side. Somebody will ferry you over, while my friend will wait for you with a car. He can take you to Guangzhou Railway Station and have your tickets ready,' Roger explained.

'Do you know how long it takes to get a passport?' JJ asked.

'I don't know, but probably not less than three or four weeks.'

JJ's heart sank as he thought about his appointment in Shanghai. 'I would like to contact Fred's brother in Shanghai. Can you help us with that?'

'I think it would be best to first get Fred into China, so we do not alert the Chinese authorities. Communications from abroad are likely to be intercepted.'

JJ's lips tightened, but his expression remained polite.

'Let's talk about the details later on. Our food is arriving. Let's enjoy our dinner,' Roger said, averting any further questions that JJ was about to ask.

Fred took the chance to cut in and JJ summarised for him.


They chose a tarte Tatin for dessert, and they served it with whipping cream and vanilla ice-cream.

'This is a real luxury. Cream and ice,' Roger said, taking a spoonful with a contented smile.

'Now, to go back to our topic, if I help your friend, I would like your friend to help me too,' he said. 'I need to collect a parcel in Changsha and pass it to someone in Shanghai. As you need to change train in Changsha, it would work out very well. You can get the parcel and spend the night in the city, before getting the train to Shanghai. Once there, I need you to take the parcel to someone directly.'

'A parcel? What is it?' JJ asked.

'Something my friend and I bought in China,' Roger

said.

JJ expected Roger to say more, but instead he called the waiter to complain about the small portion they got.

After dinner, they walked towards the waterfront and after passing the colonial building of the Hong Kong Club, they headed for the Star Ferry Pier.

'Let's take the ferry to Tsim Sha Tsui. We can go to the Mong Kok bazaar. You'll like it,' Roger said.

'What's at the bazaar?' JJ asked.

'It's where people with little money go to buy stuff, eat, and have fun.'

They bought tickets for the upper deck to enjoy the view of Hong Kong Island from the ferry. Once on the other side, they walked from the pier to Nathan Road, the major thoroughfare where hundreds of Chinese shop signs hung above the vehicles and pedestrians, often overlapping.

The trio passed in front of the Shui Yuet Temple on Shantung Street, a low building a few metres wide, with an arched entrance and two window-like openings on each side. JJ would have liked to go in, but Roger urged them to walk farther up to the busy section where the market started.

'It looks like a flea market,' JJ said.

'Yeah, except that in France, you would not find fortune tellers and curios like this,' Fred said, picking up a dried seahorse from a basket.

'They used these for Chinese medicine. They have lots of weird ingredients in their concoctions. Tastes disgusting, but it works,' Roger explained.

The wide-ranging choice of food was even more stunning than what the two friends saw the previous day, each stall selling an endless choice of skewers, noodles, and meat soups, the smell of fried food mixing with the faint fragrance of incense from the nearby temple.

They bought fresh fruits on skewers and slowly left the market, heading towards the darker streets, which were blissfully quiet. They were not walking haphazardly; Roger knew that a couple of streets west of the market, there was a hidden courtyard leading to a private opium den. A triad member he used to know managed it.

At the door, he knocked and a slender Chinese man of indeterminable age promptly opened it.

'Luojie sinsaang, welcome back,' he said, and he led Roger to a side room. 'You body pain? Bad dreams?'

'Today I brought you guests, Old Huang. Give us a good room and a good strong pipe.'

Old Huang called an attendant and gave him instructions.

'I think you both could do with something to relax. Come on,' Roger said to JJ and Fred.

'What's this smell?' Fred asked, making a face.

JJ recognised the smell immediately. 'I think it's opium.'

'Really?' Fred said, thrilled.

JJ struggled between concern and interest, but as Roger lightly pushed him forward, he let his curiosity prevail.

The den was the antithesis of the Parisian Grill a few hours earlier. From the corridor, JJ and Fred saw a large room with bamboo mats covering a dusty floor. Everywhere were bodies lying on the mats, heads resting on wooden blocks or arms. They were brought to a private room, which was bare but as dusty as the main room.

While the attendant prepared a pipe, JJ's focus

112

floated between the black pellet warming up and his memories. The rising smell guided his thoughts to his mother, and he saw her lying on her side on the rattan couch, a pillow under her head. He looked at her loose trousers, the bright red ones with golden tigers; he liked the pattern, but he hated it when she wore them because he knew she would lie there for several hours without moving. He was not allowed to disturb her that day, nor the day after, when she would wear sunglasses even inside the house. The maid would shadow her and constantly inviting her to drink another glass of coloured water. Father was never home on those occasions; it was just him and his mother. JJ felt even lonelier and excluded on those days; he ate his meals alone, and George could visit. Upon his father's return, his mother would be her old self again, cheerful and smiling. Maybe she would organise a dinner partyha with the newly arrived foreigners or teach in the nuns' school. Even George would show up.

'I haven't seen you for a few days. What did you do?' George would ask, visiting JJ after school.

'Nothing really. I stayed in to keep my mother company. She always feels a little sad when my father is not here,' JJ said, somehow unwilling to share his mother's strange behaviour.

George would shrug and show JJ the latest butterfly he caught.

Funnily enough, JJ was now presented with another butterfly, this time painted in pastel colours on the bowl of the opium pipe. The attendant waited until he took his first inhalation.

Fred looked relaxed and at ease, and JJ was sure that with each pull, his friend's mind would drift away, letting his vivid imagination come up with more stories and adventures, in which he would be obviously the acclaimed hero.

'Do you come often here?' JJ asked Roger, who had not yet started smoking.

'I come regularly. You are too young, but the war was not a pleasant affair here. The experience in the POW camp left me with back pain. I found that opium is a better companion than alcohol. At least you are at less of a risk of picking a fight with a triad member,' Roger said with a laugh.

'You were a prisoner?' JJ asked, his speech now slow.

'I was. Sometimes one wonders if it is better to be a prisoner or die.' Roger took the pipe and pulled. He sighed with pleasure. 'Good stuff.'

'Is this what you want to bring to Shanghai? Drugs?' JJ asked.

'No,' Roger replied. 'China sells opium to get foreign cash, but does not let the drugs circulate. Here in Hong Kong, the traffic is controlled by the triads, and I would be a dead man if I get involved in it.' He took another pull. 'It is a jade helmet, a kind of armour for the head or so,' he continued. 'It is ancient and the person in Shanghai is a keen collector.'

Fred seemed to come alive from his motionless state as JJ briefly told him what Roger said. 'See, JJ. Roger is no drug dealer,' he said, causing JJ to blush.

'I never said he was,' JJ tried to tell Fred, who was lying on the stinky bamboo mat enjoying his smoke.

JJ felt Roger observing him, but the dutchman kept a straight face and did not comment.

'If your buyer is a collector, the piece is probably valuable. Isn't it more appropriate to use a postal service? It would be safer,' JJ ventured.

'I have reasons to believe that the piece is not totally

clean, and using a postal service could be a problem, especially if they lose the parcel,' Roger explained.

They fell silent and concentrated on smoking. After a few more minutes, JJ felt his consciousness melt and reality drift away.

JJ only realised he had passed out when he felt liquid flowing down his face. He opened his eyes to see Roger holding a cup of water in one hand while shaking him with the other.

'Wake up, time to go home,' Roger said. 'Help me with your friend.'

JJ's brain only registered the heaviness of his limbs when he tried to get up. He saw Roger's mouth moving, but the words that came out were a faint, distant echo. His face looked distorted like the dragons he saw in his smoky dreams.

\*\*\*

The next day, JJ and Fred woke up to the smell of coffee. Roger poured two cups of the light brownish liquid and handed them over.

JJ thanked him with a silent nod. He recalled the previous night, when he had promised he would make up his mind about Roger's request by the morning. He spent a good part of the night tossing and turning, thinking of ways to protect Fred from the risks while keeping his promises to Old Min. He dreamt of a mysterious intervention from somewhere which would allow them to get new passports quickly and with no hassle. He thought about his father, who had so many connections; maybe one call to the French Commission could solve all their problems. Should he call his parents? He thought it was worth a try, maybe.

Roger and Fred waited eagerly for him to speak, both pairs of eyes fixed on his face.

Finally, Roger could not hold it in any more. 'So, are you going to the French Commission or you want to go with your friend here? I need to know.'

JJ kept sipping his coffee. He knew he had decided. Though everything seemed to point in one direction, he still felt uncertain. He lowered his cup. He closed his eyes and took a couple of deep breaths. He recalled the last time a simple decision had such tremendous consequences in his life. He had let his mother down by leaving George alone. He had let George die. His joyful, funny, and cheerful cousin, so similar to Fred in many ways; both sought adventure and both were excited about life. JJ had to make the right decision this time. He was no longer a selfish child. He was a grown man who could stand by his promises and stand by his friends.

# Chapter 15

Roger found a phone booth on a street corner and called Cai Jun.

'Lao Cai, you didn't call back.'

'I busy. Tell me again, who are to come over?'

'It's two French guys. They have no passport. You need to arrange train tickets for them, from Guangzhou to Changsha, and then from Changsha to Shanghai, as well as an overnight stay. I also need you to pick them up at the border. When do you think we can make it?' Roger asked.

'Train tickets Guangzhou no problem, I buy. In Changsha, I know somebody. The sister of wife of my brother live Changsha, I ask her to help. She pick them at station and bring back day after for train to Shanghai.'

'How can we arrange the transfer of the helmet?'

Roger's question was met with silence. Then Cai Jun spoke again. 'Gang can get them. They go hotel next to station in private room, they can do deal,' suggested Cai Jun.

'Okay, sounds good. And this woman can pick them up afterwards there, in the hotel?' Roger asked.

'Yes, yes, no problem. It's same.'

Roger asked again about the day.

'Let's see,' Cai Jun said. 'When I get train tickets. No big problem, I can come anytime to pick them at border. But make sure this time you go to left, the spot there quite dark, and guards often too lazy to walk all way there. But late, maybe three of morning, this time guards often eyes closed.'

After agreeing to call again in a couple of days, Roger hung up the phone.

***

After taking the Star Ferry across the harbour to the Kowloon side, JJ and Fred walked down Nathan Road and found the department store Roger told them to go to. Roger had given them a roll of banknotes to buy new clothes and whatever they would need for their trip.

'It's on me. Buy nice stuff, especially the luggage. You must look respectable,' Roger had said, then he dropped them off at the Star Ferry Pier before making an important phone call.

The Cheong Hing Store was in a colonial building embellished with arcades that offered cool shade on hot days; above the arcades were two additional floors with arched windows. The worn façade, showing the passing of time, had been blackened by a fire during the war. Inside, the store sold a mishmash of products, ranging from shaving foam and brilliantine to underwear and riding clothes.

The two friends each bought a pair of trousers, two shirts, some oversized underwear, and a pair of Bermuda shorts. They laughed the first time they saw policemen wearing Bermudas with white knee-high socks, but the weather was quite warm, and they decided that if they both wore them, they would look less foolish.

After shopping, they went to the restaurant next door, which, they soon realised by the pictures on the walls, was owned by an American ex-soldier, an immense man who needed two chairs to sit in. Glad to be able to read the menu, they ordered two burgers and two Cokes.

'You have been so quiet the whole morning. Are you

worried, JJ?' Fred asked, tired of his friend's uncommunicative mood.

'I am. Are you not? Don't you think they might shoot us when we cross the border?'

'Oh no, I trust Roger. He is a cool guy, and he seems to know all sorts of things and people, like my brother.' Fred was perplexed that JJ was still suspicious of Roger. He really thought the Dutch was like Marcel, even though Fred could not understand much of what he said. Roger had the same charm his brother had, and Fred could clearly see people respected him.

'You trust Roger? How can you trust him? He wants to use us as his courier,' JJ said, widening his eyes.

'But he said in the den that it was not drugs, right?' Fred was actually secretly happy to have a mission to accomplish, too.

'That's what he said, but how can we be sure? And he said that the goods are not clean. It probably means they're stolen goods,' JJ said.

'JJ, I was thinking… Roger wants the jade helmet to sell, I suppose,' Fred said.

'I think so, yes. Why?'

'Well, then it means he must have contacts here in art galleries.' Excited, Fred spilled a little Coke from his glass. 'Don't you think he can help you sell the painting of your teacher?'

JJ looked sceptical, but he agreed that the idea was not far-fetched.

'Wouldn't it be great? We get to Shanghai, we get our passports, you get your urn, the scroll, and through Roger, you sell it in a blink of an eye. You can keep both your promise and fulfil your mission in one go,' Fred said, congratulating himself for giving his friend his fantastic idea.

'The question is whether we will get to Shanghai

alive,' JJ said.

'But didn't you hear what Roger said? He said that foreigners will not be stopped. And with our nice clothes and this elegant piece of luggage we bought,' Fred said, lifting a rectangular case with a brown-and-white chequered pattern, 'we will look like two young men discovering the world together.'

'I don't know. Maybe I should go to the French Commission this afternoon. Or I could call my father. He might help me and get me a passport on the spot. Maybe my father could help you get one too,' JJ said.

Fred pulled a face like a child who has been asked to eat vegetables.

'Your brother might be mad at you for missing the boat, but you won't need to tell him that the passport is fake and… '

'Listen, you don't need to come. Nobody is forcing you. I can go alone to China. I will manage,' Fred said, his voice a little louder, his back straight, and his posture alert, as if ready for a fight.

'Fred, I'm trying to be reasonable here. I reflected upon the risks again and I think you underestimate them. You don't even speak English. I am worried about you going alone,' JJ said.

'If you're worried, then come with me! A real friend would be ready to help a friend in need,' Fred said, keeping his tone belligerent. He noticed JJ's anguish but refused to acknowledge it.

'I am your friend, but I thi—'

'I would do it for you, you know,' Fred interrupted. 'If you had no passport, and you wanted to cross the border anyway, I would cross it with you, no matter what.'

JJ remained silent.

The waitress brought the two ice creams they had

ordered after their meals. Fred grabbed a spoon and attacked the dessert, his anger churning in the soft cream.

'Fred, this is serious business. If we get caught—'

'We won't get caught! And don't you want to meet your teacher's daughter? I am sure we'll be fine. I read once a book about a spy and I learned a few tricks,' Fred said, helping himself to another spoon of ice cream. 'For example, we can use different names. I think I'd like to be called Humphrey, like Humphrey Bogart… or James Dean!' He was looking at a few portraits hanging in the restaurant. 'No, even better! You are Humphrey and I am James! Yes, with your serious face and quiet attitude, you resemble Bogart. What do you think?' Fred finished, whirling his spoon in the air.

'I think you are out of your mind,' JJ said, massaging his temples.

JJ wondered whether the dull headache he felt since that morning was because of the opium or to the mess he had in his head. Fred was right. He did not want to miss the meeting with Old Min's daughter, and getting a passport would take too long. Going with Fred offered him a shortcut. He knew he could find another solution, if he really had to, but the more Fred kept daydreaming, the more JJ felt terrified his friend might get into trouble. It had been such a long time since he had a friend his age. Fred made him laugh; they could enjoy themselves like children, and this was something he missed in his childhood: a companion. He decided to take one step at a time: first the border crossing, then the trip to Shanghai, then the selling of the scroll.

\*\*\*

It was only two more days before they would cross the border, and Roger was teaching JJ a few words of

Cantonese. He also tried to teach Fred, but he did not seem to have much talent for languages and his accent was so horrible—no Chinese could ever understand him. JJ showed more predisposition for languages, but he had a bad habit of eating the ending of words, which in Chinese would completely change the meaning. Not being fluent in Chinese could either be a blessing or a curse for them.

The day before leaving, Roger took them to the Peninsula Hotel for one of its famous afternoon tea dances, which drew the foreign community eager to mix with wealthy locals. Fred surprised his companions with his dancing skills, and left JJ and Roger alone at the table to drink their English ales as he swung on the dance floor.

'The lad is a disaster with languages, but he can dance, apparently,' Roger said, amused.

'Yes, he's very good. I didn't know that.'

'It's good that you are travelling with him, JJ. I believe you can pull this off nicely. Your friend alone might not be able to.'

JJ listened and wondered what Roger would have done, had he decided not to follow Fred. He realised he had an advantage and Fred's suggestion was worth exploring after all.

'So, you sort of owe me one?' JJ ventured.

Roger put down his beer glass, tilted his head, and gave JJ a curious look. 'I would not go that far. But it looks like you need something?'

JJ tried to shake his head in denial.

'I had a brother more or less your age. I always knew when he wanted something from me,' Roger said, taking a sip of his beer. 'So, spit it out.'

'A friend asked me to collect something in China and

sell it. It is not stolen; it belongs to him. But he cannot sell it there. He is now dead, you see. But he asked me to sell it and give the money to his daughter in Shanghai,' JJ explained.

'Aha, interesting. What is it?'

'A painting, a scroll… by a painter who is now well known.'

Roger did not bother to ask the name, and JJ thought that he knew as little as he did about Chinese painters.

'I tell you what. You sell the helmet and get the money, and I help you sell your painting and get the money.'

'So, if I do not sell the helmet, you will not help sell the scroll?'

'Why would I? Are we splitting the money in half?'

JJ swiped his hand in the air and said, 'I can't. The money does not belong to me.'

'I wash your hands, you wash mine; this is how it works, JJ,' Roger said.

'But you are asking more of me. I am taking risks by selling stolen things.'

'Not 'things', only one. You are free to choose. I am not forcing you to do anything. But if you go,' he started, as he leaned in towards JJ, 'just to make things clear… If you go, I expect to see the money.'

'Of course, who do you think I am? I am just worried about the border crossing and the sale. What if something goes wrong?' This question had been bothering JJ in the last few days.

'I crossed the border like this a few times, and the risks are minimal. As for the sale, I trust my friend to have it organised so that the handover of the object will happen with little hassle. You just make sure you keep your story straight if someone asks why you are there, and keep an eye on your luggage,' Roger said, relaxed.

'Why would someone go to that city? What's the

name? Changsha?'

'I don't know. I guess for its temples? They are everywhere in China.'

Roger's confidence failed to reassure JJ. On the contrary, Roger's trust in him placed a heavier burden on JJ. He thought it was somewhat unfair that he was in this mess because of Fred. Had he not left the ship to visit Hong Kong with Fred, he would be in Shanghai. Still, he recognised that the crossing was his only chance to get to Shanghai to keep his appointment with Old Min's daughter. And most of all, he did not want to disappoint his friend in need. Yes, he could pull this off, and then Roger would help him sell the scroll. It was all going to go well, wasn't it?

# Chapter 16

'It's nine o'clock. We won't leave before two or three am. Get some sleep first,' Roger said to JJ and Fred on the night of the crossing. 'I will wake you up.'

To his surprise, JJ found he could fall asleep easily, while Fred seemed quite agitated. During dinner, he kept asking Roger to take them to the opium den again. Roger had refused without hesitation. 'You need to be awake and alert. This is not a time to smoke.' After that, Fred made a long face and did not speak a word for the rest of the evening.

Instead of sleeping himself, Roger lit a cigarette and took a cold beer from his fridge. He had organised everything as efficiently as he could, but too much was out of his control: travelling in the cover of darkness meant the junk would be hidden from the sea patrol, but it would also make it difficult for Cai Jun to see the men when they reached the shore.

The fisherman Roger had contacted to help him was an old acquaintance, Lao Wang, a well-known boatman who offered his services to the highest bidder. He was a jovial man, smiling with all his teeth, with a sharp brain and quick thinking. Roger had heard more than one story about how he had played dumb when necessity arose. His experience was going to be crucial for the success of the crossing. But after that, and after leaving Guangzhou, the Frenchmen were going to be on their own, with little help. Roger jotted down his address and the phone number of his parents on a piece of paper for JJ. If something went wrong, then…

\*\*\*

One o'clock. JJ woke up with a start because of some noise coming from the street. He saw that it was not yet time for their crossing, but noticed that both Fred and Roger were finally asleep.

Two o'clock. The alarm clock reverberated in the room as if it were a bomb, and all three occupants of the flat jumped out of their beds. They had gone to sleep dressed in the clothes they would wear out, as if expecting to flee at any moment. A few minutes after the alarm rang, they were all ready to go.

They took a car to the harbour, where the junk was waiting for them. The two friends looked with apprehension at the frail body of the boat; it was like those they had seen at Aberdeen, half of the boat was covered. Roger planned to leave the two friends in the hands of Lao Wang, but at the last moment, he decided to go with them to ensure that all was well. He would not need to go ashore and planned to return to Hong Kong with the boatman immediately. Lao Wang complained as that was not the arrangement, but with the promise of more cash, he agreed to take him on board, too.

Roger climbed aboard first, followed by JJ, who could hold himself steady enough; Fred tumbled in, causing the boat to rock and all three of them to hold each other's arms to find their balance. Roger led the two friends inside the covered alcove, which contained a bed, a small cabinet, and a couple of pictures of the owner. JJ and Fred sat down, their faces slowly getting their colour back.

126

'Will it hold us to our destination?' JJ asked.

'If it does not, we will have to swim,' was Roger's reply.

'Are there sharks here or anything like that?' It was Fred's turn to ask.

'Yes, and they are especially fond of French food,' Roger said, laughing out loud with JJ.

A second later, Fred joined them, unsure if it was a joke.

*\*\**

Roger looked up at the sparse clouds in the night sky. The moonlight could reach the junk in patches and it was bright enough to let the sea patrol spot their boat, if they happened to be doing their rounds.

Lao Wang was rowing with constant strokes, the pole rhythmically dipping in and out of the sea, and the junk spraying and splashing, and lulling its passengers. The quiet atmosphere contrasted with the mood onboard. Fred looked like he wanted to talk, but Roger's stern expression discouraged him, thus he just sat and sighed to himself. Roger, meanwhile, was stretching his back, making it pop and hiss in all directions; he looked like a snake being teased by a stick.

The boat was pushing forward at such a slow speed that JJ, who was a good swimmer, thought he could have swum faster than the boat. JJ's hands were shaking, and he hid the light tremor by rubbing them together, as if they were cold. He tried to distract himself by watching the others. Roger's back was turned to him, and JJ noticed a few drops of sweat on his nape. Fred had stopped sighing and, eyes closed, he almost looked asleep but for his fidgeting that betrayed his nerves.

JJ unconsciously held each of his breaths longer than

usual, as if *not* breathing meant they were not going to be discovered. Sweat run down his back too, despite the cool temperature. The pit of his stomach contracted, sending pangs of pain across his body. He tried to resist the waves of aches, but it was a futile effort that brought no relief. After a few minutes, sweat continued to flow out of every pore.

The Hong Kong–China border was a porous one and the navy frigates patrolling the sea had an especially tough job. Occasionally, only a local petty officer was on board, making it easier for smugglers to cross. The worst was when it was an English petty officer with grand dreams of achieving a brilliant career in the Royal Navy. His inexperience and eagerness made the officer dangerous, and there had been a few incidents in the past, where junks had been sunk and its patrons left at sea.

On the Chinese side, the guards were not as well equipped, and it was widely known that around the time Roger had arranged their boat to be in Chinese waters, the guards would mostly be asleep.

Roger looked at his watch. 'Only a few miles left, in half an hour, maybe twenty minutes, we are in Chinese waters,' he said, grinding his teeth.

His unusual tone made JJ look closely at him. 'Roger, you are very pale. Are you unwell?'

'My back… ' He tried to move but could barely budge a centimetre.

JJ and Fred hurried to his side and tried to slide a pillow under his lower back.

Roger opened his eyes as an unexpected flash of light hit the boat. Outside, someone was shouting into a megaphone in Cantonese to stop the boat. JJ and Fred sucked in their breath, and they turned to Roger with their eyes wide open.

'Stay calm, the boatman will halt, I told him to do so,

in case they found us. The police will come on board and will tell us to row back,' Roger said.

JJ and Fred looked unsure when they heard the first shot, which luckily only hit the water. Going against Roger's instructions, the junk was not stopping. Roger cursed Lao Wang in Cantonese, but his voice was not loud enough. He tried again to move, but the pain was too excruciating. JJ and Fred, their hands squeezed together, could see by then that a layer of fear had veiled Roger's face.

'I cannot swim,' Fred said in a fluster to JJ.

JJ squeezed Fred's hands tighter.

Another shot, another miss, but this time it got much closer.

Roger kept yelling in vain to Lao Wang, asking him to stop the boat. The boatman shouted something, and right after, another pair of feet ran along the junk, reaching the pole on the stern, and started rowing from there. They had company. Lao Wang had brought somebody else on board. It was then clear to Roger why Lao Wang did not want to stop the boat. He was transporting something illegal, and he had no wish to get caught or lose the goods.

'Faster, faster!' Roger shouted, his voice like thunder in the otherwise silent cabin. The boat picked up pace, the additional rower obviously younger than Lao Wang. The shots seemed to sound farther away, but they still resonated like thunder, too close to the territory of the Chinese guards. JJ feared the shots would wake the guards on the other side.

Then the shooting ceased. They were in Chinese waters. The boat was now moving fast, and the occupants were straining their ears for any Chinese boats. Nothing. Only silence. The stillness of the three men in the cabin was now matched by that outside. They all breathed more easily, but still did not dare say a word. The diversion had caused their boat to deviate from its original course. JJ felt the boat stop and wait, then it turned and went in a different direction, towards the arranged meeting point. By now, the sky had switched off its starlight and a timid sunrise was emerging amid the clouds and early mist.

# Chapter 17

On the Chinese coast, Cai Jun looked worried. They were late. The sun was already rising. He grumbled to himself as he realised he could not possibly go to his flat with two foreigners in broad daylight, as his nosy neighbours were always alert. The railway was station not a safe place either, especially as they were carrying so much money. None of the options looked good. He grabbed his pack of cigarettes, but found it empty. So he woke up the driver next to him and asked him for one.

A minute later, Cai Jun got out of the car, lit his cigarette, and walked closer to the coastal rocks. In the faint dawn light, he could now scan the horizon for approaching boats. Finally, one came into sight. He saw the junk dock and two men secure it with a rope. But no foreigners emerged. One boatman climbed the lower cliffs and walked towards him. Cai Jun recognised the man as he came closer. They had met once before.

'The lǎowài is sick. You pay me, and you come to pick him up. Otherwise I throw him in the water,' he said to Cai Jun.

'The foreigner is sick? Which one? What does it have?'

'The old foreigner. I don't know. He cannot move. You pay me, you pick him up. I will not take him back to Hong Kong.'

Cai Jun called the driver, and they went to the junk. Entering the boat alcove, Cai Jun saw two youthful faces looking lost and upset while Roger was lying down and seemed to be in severe pain.

'Luojie, how you feel, where is pain?' he asked Roger.

'My back. I cannot move,' Roger answered through clenched teeth.

'Luojie, boatman want his money and not want bring you back. Dim sü? What we do?'

Cai Jun saw Roger was in no condition to decide. He paid the boatman and carried Roger to the car with the help of the driver and the two young foreigners. They laid him on the car's rear seat; Cai Jun and the driver sat in front, while the other two squatted somehow in the back with Roger.

Starting the car, the driver turned to Cai Jun. 'Where are we going? Not to your flat, are we?'

Pointing his chin forward, Cai Jun said, 'Let's move first. I will think about it on the way. It will take at least a couple of hours before we get there.' He looked back at Roger and frowned. Roger was in and out of consciousness, and his back pain was complicating things: Cai Jun needed to find a place for the three lǎowài to stay and a doctor.

Cai Jun reached for his driver's cigarettes for the umpteenth time. The thick silence was interrupted only by moans from the back each time the car hit a pothole. Cai Jun turned to make sure their heads were not visible through the windows. Guangzhou was approaching; the car passed over the Pearl River as it headed north.

The driver peeked in the rear-view mirror and commented on how the foreigners had once invaded Guangzhou. 'And now look. One is sick, the other two are crawling like chickens laying eggs,' he said with a chuckle.

'Right,' said Cai Jun as the city landscape emerged before them, 'but they left some beautiful buildings for us. Look at Shamian.' Of course! Shamian. He slapped the dashboard with his hand and turned to the driver. 'Drive to the church in Shamian. There are missionaries. They are supposed to help people in need. We'll go there.'

***

The driver parked the car next to a small church. The streets were deserted, so Cai Jun let JJ and Fred out to stretch while he went off to find the parson. It took him a while to find the right door. It was locked, so he banged on it vigorously. Nothing. He was about to swear under his breath at the laziness of foreigners when the door opened, revealing a tall white man in a black gown. He looked to be in his fifties.

'Shénfù, Father, sorry to bother you. I wonder if you would help me. I have three lǎowài in the car. It is not convenient to have them at my place. The two young men, I will take them to the train station this afternoon. The older man is not well, cannot move.'

The parson listened without interrupting.

'Can you understand me?' Cai Jun asked.

'Take him to the hospital. I am not a doctor,' he replied.

'Please, Father, help. I don't speak the language of the young men and the old man is very sick. They have no documents. If I go to the hospital, it is a problem.'

The parson took in the situation: one middle-aged smuggler, two disciples, and a Chinese scoundrel. He had to be careful. The relationship between the Chinese government and the Church was not an easy one. Since the end of the civil war in 1949, many missionaries had left the country and only a handful were left, mostly those belonging to the Protestant church under the Three-Self Patriotic Movement. He hesitated, then he accompanied Cai Jun to the car to meet the three foreigners.

'Good morning, sirs. You seem to be in trouble?' he said to JJ and Fred in English.

Flustered, the two friends shook his hand and mumbled a shy good morning.

'Ah, vous êtes français!' he said, recognising their accent from their first hello. 'Call me Kurt.'

JJ's and Fred's faces lit up at hearing him speak French.

'Lovely country, France. I spent quite a long time in the south during the war. My wife is French,' he said, speaking the language fluently, but in an accent as heavy as Fred had when he spoke the two words of English he knew.

Father Kurt noticed their scepticism. 'Ah non, I am not German, je suis Suisse, I am Swiss.'

Father Kurt looked in the car and saw Roger, who by now was soaked with sweat. 'What is your problem, sir?' he asked, switching back to English.

'My back hurts. I need painkillers and a place to rest for a few days,' Roger said.

'Oh, well, glad to see it is a minor, even though clearly painful, matter,' Father Kurt said with half a smile. 'I was expecting a gunshot wound or something similar... With all the smugglers along the coast, you never know.'

He gestured to Cai Jun and the driver to take Roger inside, then motioned JJ and Fred to follow them.

They carried Roger inside the flat and a woman, taking in the scene, promptly hurried to open the door to a guest room.

'Yvette, please bring him a painkiller,' Father Kurt told the woman.

She nodded and left the room, opening a passage between JJ and Fred, who were standing at the door of the guest room.

As Father Kurt invited the two friends to sit outside in the living room, she returned with the pills and a glass of water for Roger and disappeared into the guest room. JJ looked with some curiosity at the young woman as she came out again to fetch more glasses of water for everyone. She looked closer in age to him and Fred than to her husband. Her brown hair matched her eyes, and her long neck reminded him of Modigliani's paintings; she was definitively very French in her appearance but far from being a classical beauty. Still, her slow movements and her silent, almost solemn expression radiated calm and peace, like Raphael's Madonna. JJ looked at his hands; they had stopped trembling, but he felt his body was still full of adrenaline. He almost wanted to ask the young woman to lend him an ounce of her calm.

Cai Jun stood by the bed and looked ready to leave. 'Father, many thanks for your help,' he said. 'Here, take this for the inconvenience.' He offered Father Kurt a few bills. 'I come to pick up the young men later in the afternoon. Can you tell them?'

Father Kurt took the money with a firm hand and looked at JJ and Fred. 'I have to get ready for Mass. Yvette can prepare some breakfast for you. Are you tired? Do you need to sleep?'

'I'll pass on the food, thank you. My stomach is still upset from the boat trip and then the car... ' JJ said.

135

Fred nodded in agreement.

'Yes, one wonders whether it is the road which is bad, or the car. But more often than not, it's both of them combined,' Father Kurt replied, and laughed.

They had no other spare room, so he asked his wife to make up the bed in their bedroom and let the young men sleep there.

Yvette disappeared, unhurried, to make the bed. She opened the wardrobe, where the bed linen was stored on one side and her husband's dark robes on the other. Her own clothes were arranged in the chest of drawers, on top of which were framed pictures of her husband and herself, back in France, of his parents in Switzerland, and of his friends from his time at the seminary. She had no pictures of herself from before the marriage. No friends, no family, no money.

She spread the sheets on the bed, with more energy than usual, lost in her thoughts. Then she smoothed her hair and her dress before returning to the living room.

'Voilà, the bed is ready. You can close the door, but I warn you, it will get somewhat sticky. You better turn on the ceiling fan,' she said to the two men, paying attention to her voice so that it was neither too high nor too low.

'Thank you, we won't disturb you for too long. We will take the train this afternoon,' JJ said.

She looked at him, startled. 'This afternoon? Where are you going? What about your friend? He does not look like he can move.'

'He is not leaving with us,' Fred replied. 'We are going to Shanghai.'

'I see. Then get some rest now. I shall wake you up for lunch, so that you can have a good meal before leaving. I will also ask our maid to prepare something for the train.' Not even her husband could have picked up the slight disappointment in her voice.

JJ and Fred closed the bedroom door and threw themselves onto the bed.

'Boy, what a night!' Fred said to the ceiling. 'When I heard the gunshot, I almost pissed in my pants.'

'Yes,' echoed JJ, 'I was paralysed, and I could barely breathe. My mind was completely blank, and I had the impression that each shot had hit the boat!'

'Yes,' said Fred, in an excited, high-pitched voice. 'And then, thinking we were at sea, we could not run, so we fall into the water, drown... ' He shook his head to remove the images from his mind.

'Yes,' JJ said.

They glanced at each other, then laughed aloud, relieving the pressure that had held them hostage for so long. Soon after, they fell asleep, forgetting everything for the moment, even forgetting to turn on the ceiling fan.

# Chapter 18

After Mass, Father Kurt went to look for Doctor Yang, a small man with thick glasses and a missing finger in his right hand. Doctor Yang was not a churchgoer and, like many Chinese, he was wary of Father Kurt. But he had a reputation of being a conscientious doctor and discreet, and more than once had come to the parish to treat Father Kurt or Yvette.

At Roger's bedside, Doctor Yang sat close to the patient on a wooden chair partially eaten by worms. He noticed that Roger's right ear was imperceptibly closer to the head than the left one, a telling mark of someone with an opium habit. The eyes were not too bloodshot, however, which showed that his smoking still fell short of being an addiction. His wiry pulse and the redness on his tongue hinted at Qi stagnation and emotional strain. The doctor had seen many similar cases, and he concluded that Roger's back pain was a result of the Qi stagnation, and the war, of course.

'I do not have medicine for you,' Doctor Yang told Roger. 'I can offer you only an acupuncture treatment for the pain.'

'No! You crazy Chinese doctors, wanting to sting any living soul to death. I won't have it,' Roger said. 'I prefer the pain.' His booming voice was again at full strength, thanks to the painkiller. 'Chinese medicine is all fake.'

'Then I cannot help. I do not know where the problem in your back is, without a proper exam in a hospital. I can only help you subdue the pain.'

Towering over the bed, Father Kurt tried to persuade

Roger. 'Western drugs and painkillers are scarce these days. We brought our own reserve from Europe and there is not much left. If your pain continues, we have nothing to help you.' He spoke in the same tone he used for his sermons.

'I can pay you; I can send you some painkillers from Hong Kong when I get back. I won't let him pierce me. No way.' Roger was almost shouting now, rising and propping himself up on his elbow to confront the parson.

'Yang dàifū, can't you give him some herbs or something?' Father Kurt asked, looking for an alternative.

'Herbs won't help much with the pain, and would take a long time to have any effect, at least six weeks. Does he want to wait six weeks?' replied the doctor.

'Six weeks? I don't think I want to wait that long,' Father Kurt said.

He turned to Roger again. 'My dear son, you hear what he says. The doctor would like to help, I would like to help, but you need to be reasonable. You certainly do not want to spend six weeks in bed, do you? God sends us his tests, and it's in the hardship of life that we can find greatness. Look at acupuncture as a test.' Father Kurt delivered the lines with his most solemn expression, which made Roger raise his eyebrow despite the pain.

Still, Roger shook his head before lying back on the pillow again, his eyes closed. 'I need to sleep. The effect of the painkiller will end soon.'

'Yang dàifū, I am so sorry for troubling you,' Father Kurt said, walking the doctor to the front door.

Yvette was in the living room, busy mending clothes. Moths flourished in the humid weather of Guangzhou, and especially in the cold, wet winter days, when the laundry took days to dry, it was easy to find new holes in the clothing.

'So troublesome,' Father Kurt said to his wife when he returned from the door. 'The sick one does not want acupuncture; he only wants painkillers. How many do we have left?' He picked up a cup of tea his wife had prepared for him.

'Only two more,' she answered, looking up. 'You need them, too. Do you think we can find some more somewhere?'

'This man said he can send us some from Hong Kong, and the doctor said we might get some at the Guangzhou First People's Hospital.'

'So, you think we should use all our reserves?' Yvette turned her focus back to the work in her hand.

'Let's wait and see. When the effects of the first one disappear, let's make him wait before giving him the second one. That might bring him to reason. I do not want to be left without even one painkiller.' Father Kurt took a sip of his tea and stared ahead, as if concentrating on finding an answer. He had excellent health, but his rotten teeth sometimes caused him severe and sudden toothaches. He was open to trying out many things in China, but he refused to see a dentist here. Ironically, his attitude was not dissimilar to that of Roger.

'The Frenchmen are leaving this afternoon, I heard?'

'Yes, it seems they must catch a train later. Their Chinese friend, or whatever he is, is going to pick them up. Are they sleeping?' Father Kurt said.

'Yes, they are sleeping. I told them I would wake them up for lunch. I sent Xiao Lin to buy some fish at the market. Are they coming back here after their trip?' Yvette said.

'Why buy fish?' Father Kurt cut in, ignoring her

question.

Yvette looked surprised but refrained from commenting. She said instead, 'The journey by train will be exhausting. Remember when we went to Beijing?' With her hands on her lap, she turned to her husband, waiting for a reply.

Father Kurt made an inarticulate noise, between a grunt and a yes, bringing his cup to his lips. He often complained to her that his allowance was not as high as he expected and reproached his wife about the household expenses. Lost in his thoughts, he failed to hear the maid return and realised her presence only when the smell of fish pervaded the living room.

The maid had brought home two fish in a bag, which Father Kurt knew were alive and kicking just a few minutes before, and now were still weakly twitching their tails. In a moment, the maid would lower the chopper, with a sure hand, onto their heads, if she was making a soup. Otherwise, she would fry them whole in hot oil in a wok. By that time, they would already be gone to a better world. Crabs had it much worse, and Father Kurt forbade cooking them in his home, confining the pleasure of savouring them in the occasional lunches offered by other foreigners.

While the maid and Yvette were busy in the kitchen, he decided to write his monthly report. Priests were carer of souls, but also the eyes and ears of the Church. From their privileged position, they could gather all sorts of information about the society and the political mood of the place where they were posted.

In his winding calligraphy, he started writing.

*In these recent weeks, there have been fewer incidents involving local landowners or businesses,*

141

*and no remarkable events took place. Outside Guangzhou, it seems the government has started putting families together to work the land. Each family contributes a plot and reaps the produce according to the size of the plot. But the work is pooled, as are the tools. The strips of land between the plots belong to this new production unit. Maybe twenty to forty families are in a unit. I am afraid, though, that this will go further if the news from Shanghai is true. The government wants to get rid of private property and this might be a first step.*

*Premier Zhou Enlai came back from another trip to India; the relationship between the two countries seems to continue to develop. Contacts with the Soviet Union are also multiplying. In Guangzhou, the presence of several Russians has been confirmed both by a Swiss journalist who visited and by Mr Hans Guo, a Chinese-German landowner—who by the way is very worried about the development of the state of affairs and he talks about selling his land and leaving China.*

*Mr Zhou Enlai also paid a visit to Guangzhou, where he is respected and remembered fondly since his time in the political department of the Whampoa Military Academy. He was a guest at a dinner hosted by Mr Guo, which I attended, but had no chance to speak with him.*

The door of the bedroom opened, and JJ and Fred came out somewhat unkempt.

'Hello!' Father Kurt called, putting down his pen. 'Did you sleep well?'

'Yes, thank you,' Fred replied, yawning.

'Please, have a seat,' Father Kurt said. 'It is almost lunchtime. Are you hungry?'

'Oh yes, now I am starving!' said Fred, while JJ pulled up a chair, still half asleep.

Yvette came out of the kitchen, letting into the living room the tantalising smell of something frying. 'You woke up. This is good; lunch is almost ready,' she said, nodding.

JJ looked wary and foresaw that they would have to converse with Father Kurt over lunch. This had not been part of the plan. Fred, JJ, and Roger had not even agreed on their story in case they were asked why they were here. He looked at Fred, now relaxed and his usual self. JJ was most afraid of what Fred would say; he sometimes had a big mouth.

Fred asked for a toilet, and Father Kurt took him to a side room next to the kitchen. 'I am afraid this is all we can offer.'

JJ heard Fred saying he had no luck with toilettes, and he got up to have a look.

'A bedpan?' said JJ with questioning eyes.

'Well, my sons. You are lucky. In many places, you just get a hole in a field or a wooden cabin.'

'I've lost my appetite,' Fred said.

'*You*? I cannot believe it… ' JJ looked at Father Kurt and explained with a grin, 'He ate a chicken right after having seen one decapitated.'

Back in the living room, lunch was being served; on the table were two large fish, covered with orange and green stripes. In one bowl, there were green vegetables, mixed with something white; in another bowl, an unknown meat covered in a blackish sauce; then white rice; and a soup with dòufu and leafy green vegetables. Fred and Father Kurt joined JJ and Yvette at the table, forks instead of chopsticks laid out next to the plates.

JJ took some meat and vegetables and placed them

143

on top of the rice, as Yvette and Father Kurt did.

'Oh, that's a lot of garlic', he said, 'and spicy,' he added, making a face.

'Yes, we like garlic and we use it a lot, as it is supposed to be good for your health, while spicy food helps to kill germs, so they say, at least,' Father Kurt said.

'These are my favourite, eggplants with meat and chili beans. Our maid comes from a region where they eat very spicy, so she is always very generous with the chili. Indeed, it is very good to clean your intestines,' Yvette said with a smile.

JJ nodded, his tongue still burning from the intense taste.

'You are lucky. We do not use chopsticks here. Otherwise, you probably could not eat,' remarked Father Kurt.

'Actually, we can. We spent some time in Hong Kong and we ate with chopsticks,' Fred said.

*There he goes*, JJ thought.

'How come you stayed there? Are you two and your companion family members?' asked Yvette, spooning some rice into each bowl.

'No, no, we met him in Hong Kong. He is a friend, a great friend. Helped us a lot, didn't he, JJ?'

JJ told half of their story. 'Yes, we missed our boat, and Roger is helping us through his friend to reach Shanghai. As we have little money, travelling by land is cheaper,' he explained, hoping that his reply would sound plausible.

'Weird choice, though. The journey by train is certainly more interesting, but definitely more complicated, especially for foreigners. Can you speak the language?' Father Kurt asked, topping his rice with some fish.

144

'Not really. Just a few words, enough to ask for easy information though,' replied JJ, his mouth half full.

'We took the train once. We went to Beijing,' Yvette said. 'It was a long journey; you better be prepared. Which class are you travelling in?'

'We don't know, Roger's friend has our tickets,' JJ replied, thinking that it was silly not to have asked. He felt that each wrong word might reveal the real reason behind their trip.

'Hopefully the soft sleepers, then. They are more comfortable, even if less colourful. Though the journey to Shanghai will be shorter than going to Beijing, isn't it, Kurt?' She looked to her husband for confirmation, but before he could reply, Fred cut in.

'We won't be travelling directly to Shanghai. We will make a stop on the way, in another city… ' He trailed off with a questioning look and turned sharply to JJ.

JJ, looking elsewhere, gave Fred a second light kick under the table; the first kick had been more energetic and had hit his friend as he was finishing his sentence. JJ hoped he would get the signal and stop talking so much.

'Another city? Which one?' Father Kurt asked.

Both Father Kurt and Yvette stopped eating as if this piece of information were of the utmost importance to their lives, and they alternated their glances at Fred, then at JJ.

Fred avoided their looks and concentrated on mixing the rice and meat in his bowl. JJ kept moving his hands on and off the table. He felt Father Kurt's penetrating gaze.

*Merde, I was angry at Fred for talking so much but I am the one here who is looking suspicious with my behaviour*, he thought.

'I think the name is Changsha,' JJ finally said.

145

Father Kurt looked pleased with himself, seeing how his piercing look had not failed him. He was determined to find out more about the two.

'And why are you stopping there? I heard they are building a museum there and that they have an unofficial exhibition of a few artefacts. Are you interested in the history of ancient China?' Yvette asked.

JJ was glad for this suggestion and promptly replied, 'Yes… I study art and I thought it would be interesting to visit the museum.'

'Shanghai also has a museum, and it's open; it is likely to have more things to see, and nicer ones, there,' Father Kurt said, arching an eyebrow.

'The temples, I have never seen temples before, and I heard there are many in Changsha. And Fred wanted to see them too,' JJ said, giving Fred another kick under the table, lighter this time.

Fred rushed to give his support. 'Yes, yes, I've never seen a temple and would like to, very much.'

'But in Shanghai there are temples too, and in Hong Kong.'

JJ's skin became sticky as a thin veil of sweat covered his face. He hated lying. 'Roger was not interested in temples, so he did not show us any,' JJ replied, holding his breath for a brief moment.

To their relief, Father Kurt did not ask more, and Yvette, who became more talkative, carried the rest of the conversation. While Father Kurt kept to himself, JJ, Fred, and Yvette kept chatting through the lunch and early afternoon, Yvette's open manner making the atmosphere so friendly and easy that JJ told her about Indochina. Laughing and joking, they had completely forgotten about Roger, until a shout came from the adjacent room. JJ and Fred hurried to go see him.

# Chapter 19

Cai Jun arrived shortly after four pm. He, JJ, and Fred went into Roger's room and closed the door.

'Here, pills for back,' Cai Jun said, handing a small parcel to Roger.

'How did you get them?'

'Guānxì. Connections at hospital.'

With Roger acting as a translator, Cai Jun first gave the two friends a black bag; inside, there was a white jute bag of money. JJ took the bag and peeked inside.

'How much money is that? ' JJ asked.

'Not as much as the helmet is worth, ' Roger replied, 'but the sellers do not know the real value of their finding.'

Then he told them who they had to meet and the rest of the details.

'JJ, take down the address of the church and the telephone number, if they have one. It will be an additional measure should you need help. Be careful on the train. Don't leave your luggage unattended. I will let you know the name of the buyer once you are in Shanghai,' Roger said.

Cai Jun passed them money for the journey, as well as a map of Shanghai, which he somehow managed to find. He circled the address of the buyer on the map and put a cross next to the Shanghai train station.

'We have problem,' Cai Jun said. 'Ticket wrong, not today, but tomorrow.'

'What? And you are telling us just now?' Roger said.

'I now tell you, good? Your friends stay here tonight,' Cai Jun said.

Roger grunted. 'Okay, out now, all of you. I will talk to the priest.'

As expected, Father Kurt was not eager to have all three of them as guests for the night and insisted that there was no space for them.

'You can stay, Roger, but your friends must find another accommodation,' Father Kurt said.

'I will pay you tenfold what I have already given you to let the French stay here. I don't care if they sleep on the floor,' Roger said.

The generous offer worked, and Father Kurt said he could arrange some blankets in the church's sacristy.

When he came out of the room, several pairs of eyes looked at him. 'It looks like you will spend the night here,' he said.

Yvette found herself sighing, together with Cai Jun.

'Yvette, prepare a shopping list for the maid. We will need more food for tonight,' Father Kurt said. He turned to JJ and Fred with a stern expression. 'Well, as you are staying here, you can use this time to help me. I have to copy some old documents; could you handle copying a few pages for me while I go visit some parishioners?'

JJ was the first to reply yes, followed by a less eager assent from Fred.

'Could I not join you to visit your parishioners?' Fred asked. A look from JJ made him quickly take it back. 'Ah, never mind. I'll stay here with the others.'

JJ and Fred put themselves to the task while Yvette took out her Chinese exercise notebook. They worked in silence for a short while before Fred became restless.

'Isn't Chinese difficult to learn?' he asked, putting his pen down when he saw the maid come out of the kitchen with the shopping list.

'Chinese characters are like miniatures of pictures, which makes it easier to memorise, I find,' Yvette said, 'but I find the pronunciation difficult and I do not speak much. My husband is the opposite. He cannot read but he can speak.'

'You complement each other,' Fred said, getting up to move around the room.

JJ looked at him, and he knew exactly what his friend was up to.

With his hands in his pockets, Fred pointed his chin towards the maid and said, 'Does she need help to carry the bags home?'

Yvette looked at Fred with a bright smile and replied, 'That's a good idea.'

'Wait,' JJ said. 'I am not so sure, Fred. Let's ask Roger.' And he got up to go to Roger's room with Fred.

Roger was asleep, but the closed door gave them the chance to talk undisturbed.

Fred put a hand on JJ's shoulder, reassuring him. 'I've got it, pal. I will keep my mouth shut; the girl does not speak French, anyway.'

With JJ's blessing, Fred and the maid left home.

***

'I'll make some tea. Would you like some, JJ?' Yvette asked, her face slightly flushed.

'Thank you.'

'What are these documents, exactly? They look old,' JJ asked.

'Kurt said they are old reports from a French priest who stayed here many years ago.'

'It must be interesting to read them,' JJ said.

'I don't know. I never went to school. Reading is hard for me, especially that old calligraphy,' Yvette said, her cheeks now a bright pink.

JJ raised his head from the documents, curious. 'Was it the war?' he asked her, accepting her cup of tea.

'Well, my mother died in childbirth, and my father died when I was a child. After that, I lived with my maternal grandmother for a couple of years. Then she died too. I lived with different families, and thus my schooling has been very irregular. Then came the war. It was bad, but after, it was worse,' she said, her hands cupping her teacup.

'How's that?' JJ asked.

Yvette took a slow sip of the hot tea, scalding her tongue. 'Many of the men were unhappy, and violent. I did not feel safe anymore when men were around.' She fell silent, unwilling to add more.

JJ looked at her with a dismayed look.

'Don't make such a face. It is all well. I met Kurt, and I have been taken care of since then. He takes care of me and I take care of him and of the house,' she said, flashing a little smile.

'Do you like living here?' JJ asked.

Yvette looked at a point far away as she took time to answer. 'I do. Unlike you in Phnom Penh, I am fascinated by the people and the city. It is as if my brain got a kick and started functioning since I've been here. All these unfamiliar smells, colours, sounds. People give you hard stares on the street, but they also treat you with a certain regard, which I've never had before. I feel nobody judges me simply by looking at me and nobody expects me to be something other than what I am. It is weird, but I feel more accepted by the Chinese.'

'Really? I did not have that feeling back in Indochina,' JJ said.

'Maybe you were too young. But here, you know, even if you are strange, they just say it is normal, because you are a foreigner.'

'They who? The Chinese?'

'Yes, of course. When we meet with other foreigners, I am just the little wife of a priest. Nobody really pays attention to me.'

'We have that in common, then. Nobody paid attention to me either in Indochina, not even my own mother. I think she did not love me much,' JJ said, unaware that he was repeating the sad story he always played in his head.

'What kind of mother does not love her child?' Yvette asked.

'She was too busy,' JJ rushed to say. 'She was a teacher, still is now.'

'Oh, she works.'

'Yes, she started teaching when we were in Phnom Penh. Some years ago, she passed her exam to become a teacher in France.'

'An exam? She went back to school when she was old?'

'I guess. She is now forty-four, I think,' JJ said, trying to remember the number of candles on the last birthday cake.

'What did she teach there?'

'She taught French and some English, in a school run by nuns.'

He saw Yvette make a disgusted face, which he found strange, and asked why.

Yvette simply said she used to live in an orphanage run by nuns, and it had been no fun.

'Are you then not Christian?' JJ asked, turning the cup of tea in his hands.

'I'm not.'

'Strange that you are now married to a priest,' JJ said. He tilted his head to one side to look at Yvette. Underneath her nondescript appearance and measured manners, her words and half-told tale betrayed the scars, which she kept hidden deep into herself. Her age, so close to his, made JJ feel comfortable speaking to her and now, having glimpsed into her past, he felt moved at the thought that maybe her marriage had been her way to protect herself from further pain.

Yvette was conscious of JJ's look and grabbed the cup with two hands and brought it to her lips to hide the colouring of her cheek.

'Yes, I guess it is strange. But I was not given many options in my life.'

'Ah, I feel the same, somehow. I did not choose to go to Indochina. Could not choose my parents either,' JJ said, biting his lips upon remembering that Yvette had lost her parents.

'Well, there is something that we can choose,' Yvette said.

'What?' JJ asked, leaning his body slightly towards the table.

'Friends,' she said with a smile, which JJ returned with his own.

***

After dinner, Father Kurt took JJ and Fred to the sacristy, where his assistant, Lao Wu, had arranged blankets on a thin mattress in a corner. JJ and Fred greeted him with a nod as Father Kurt sang Lao Wu's praises and told them he was lucky he had an assistant who could speak a little English, besides Cantonese and Mandarin. Little did they know that JJ and Fred would also profit from the resourcefulness of Father Kurt's assistant in a not-too-distant future.

After Father Kurt left, Fred lay down with a resounding sigh. 'That was the most stressful dinner I have ever had,' he said, 'and painful.' He inspected his ankle to see whether JJ's kicks had given him bruises.

'I'm sorry. I hope your ankle is fine,' JJ said.

Fred rubbed his leg with his thumb. 'I mean, pal, you should trust me a little, you know. I get it. We are on a secret mission. I do not wish to get caught either.' Fred's rather joyful tone undercut the seriousness of his words.

'My ankle is okay,' he continued, 'but wasn't it weird that Father Kurt kept asking so many questions? Do you think he wants to report us?'

'I don't know. It seemed like he wanted to get information out of us. I do not know how much we can trust him,' JJ said.

'Shouldn't we get out of here unseen first thing in the morning? We have the money, we have the tickets. Somehow, we will reach the station. What time does the train leave?' Fred asked, thinking his idea was excellent.

JJ took out the the small slips of paper.

'It's all in Chinese,' JJ said.

'But the time is there, look. There are carts outside pulled by men. I saw them today—they are everywhere. It's a sort of taxi here, apparently. We can show the train tickets and they will take us to the station,' Fred suggested.

'I don't know if it's a good idea. We cannot leave without saying goodbye, after all,' JJ said.

'Your church tone again,' Fred said. 'JJ, you have to be more of a man. You cannot be kind to everybody, you know.' Fred started to undress to go to sleep, but an icy shiver ran down his spine, making him change his mind, and he put on his trousers again.

'I think this is the best idea. We do not want to have Father Kurt asking us more questions, do we?' Fred said, looking pointedly at JJ, convinced that his plan would save them and their mission.

JJ still looked unsure.

'Just to be clear, if Father Kurt reports us, say goodbye to the urn, your teacher's daughter, and the scroll. If you are okay with that, fine,' Fred said, and he got into the bed, turned his back on JJ, and fell immediately asleep.

# Chapter 20

When Father Kurt found the sacristy empty the next morning, he shook his head in disapproval and told Yvette not to put out breakfast for the Frenchmen. He was not all that surprised. Then he sat at the table with the last copy of the *South China Morning Post* he received intermittently from Hong Kong, his wife's sorrowful expression going unnoticed.

'Yvette, after breakfast, take the old newspapers and see if you can find anything related to Changsha and the museum. I vaguely remember that some time ago, you mentioned an article about a museum and a robbery.'

Perplexed, Yvette went straight to the sideboard and took out the old newspapers, which doubled as toilet paper when they could not find any, and placed them on the side table for her to read later.

'Do you think they are in trouble?' Yvette asked, looking at her husband, her head tilted to the right.

'I think there is a chance for us to earn some money,' Father Kurt replied, giving voice to his thoughts. He stopped short, then added, 'They crossed the border illegally.' He returned to his food, and Yvette refrained from asking more questions.

While he ate, Father Kurt recalled his conversation with Roger the night before. He had met people like Roger before: they did what they could to survive and used people to their advantage. They only took calculated risks and usually could choose the right partners for their shadowy but lucrative businesses.

'I am not smuggling anything, and neither are they,' Roger had said, when Father Kurt had brought up the unusual way they came into China. 'Everything they do is their choice. They told me they wanted to go to China, and I simply helped them the way I could.'

'I see. But what is the price you asked for?' Father Kurt was not afraid to be direct.

'Well, Father, of course, each party has to profit from the transaction. This is the law of the market.'

'Was it just money? They are so young... If you know China, you also know that any illegal actions by a foreigner could mean jail, where he would not necessarily come out.'

'They are younger than you and me, yes, but they are adults and can make their own decisions, and like anybody else, they have to deal with the consequences of their decisions,' Roger said.

'To use one's charisma and position of strength to induce somebody to do something, which he normally would not do, is also reproachable.'

'Very well, each of us will pay for our sins, and I am glad that mine is to be too charismatic, because it has served me well in life,' replied Roger.

'If I knew what they are up to, I could help them, should they be in danger.'

'They are simply travelling without passports, Father, nothing more. They left the ship without documents, then they missed the boat,' Roger had said.

Father Kurt had remained silent while Roger spoke. Now he looked at his young wife and rose to take out an old map of China he had inherited from his predecessor, Father Guglielmo. The map showed a pencil line drawn from Guangzhou to the coast; some time ago, he had used that route to collect smuggled goods for a poor family. The porous coast offered opportunities, but he did not dare take them on his own. Father Kurt wished he could smuggle more goods into China, but he was too inexperienced and uncertain to take the risks. He thus felt Roger, who obviously did not have such qualms, was sent from heaven.

Later that afternoon, Yvette's search through the newspapers was not very fruitful. She was getting tired of deciphering the Chinese characters, so she put the remaining newspapers to the side for tomorrow. She decided instead to attend to her housework, and she replaced the bed linen, finished mending what she had started, and then helped the maid with the next meal. There had been no leftovers from the previous day, so she and Xiao Lin had to prepare lunch from scratch, contrary to the usual habits. After cutting a cucumber to prepare a salad, Yvette started cooking a vegetable soup, two easy dishes she could make with little supervision. Meanwhile, Xiao Lin stir-fried water spinach with garlic. The smell of fried garlic filled the small kitchen and was reaching the other parts of the home when the telephone rang. Yvette ran to pick it up.

'Yvette?'

Her heart jumped at the familiar voice. 'JJ! Where are you?'

'We are at the station. I just want to thank you for your hospitality and say I am sorry we left so abruptly.' JJ hesitated to add any further information.

'Are you in trouble? I would like to help you.'

'I hope not, but… '

'What is it that you have to do in Changsha? My husband knows what you did,' Yvette said, lowering her voice, even though she was alone in the room.

JJ thought about what she meant, exactly. Unless Roger had told Father Kurt about the helmet, he could not know the whole story, could he?

'Listen, whatever it is,' Yvette said, 'I can keep an eye on him to make sure he does not cause you trouble. Can you try to call me when you get to Changsha?'

JJ promised, and he felt somehow relieved to have found a friend in Yvette. At the same time, he worried about Father Kurt and what he knew.

\*\*\*

When JJ and Fred had entered the train station a few hours earlier, they found passengers and large bags and cartons crammed into every corner. People were fighting for space, breathing on each other's neck, cheeks, and heads; babies were getting half squashed between women's breasts and the backs of others; older children who were not as tall as the adults were in an even worse position, and received little air but all the bodily smells. The floor of the station was covered with white and black husks of seeds, cigarettes butts, paper, food remains, and unknown liquids.

Without being able to communicate, JJ and Fred found someone to guide them through the station, and together they walked past the mix of people to reach a room that was much quieter and not even half as full as the other parts of the station. They obviously had the best tickets, which allowed them the special treatment. From the window, they could see the train and found it unusual that passengers were asked to wait inside a room when the train was already at the platform.

During their long wait, JJ nipped off to call Yvette briefly, but other than that, they had nothing to do but observe the other passengers. They were quiet in

158

appearance, but when speaking, they were loud, as if they were fighting. Many were holding jars with a yellow liquid inside, which they would drink from time to time.

'They are not drinking urine, are they?' Fred asked. 'It cannot be, can it? I mean, one guy maybe, but there are so many doing the same.'

'You are right, but why are they drinking from a jar?' JJ asked.

Suddenly, they heard someone shout Fred's name. They turned and saw Roger's friend, Cai Jun.

'Why you go alone? Very stupid,' he told them, subtly checking whether they had the bag with them. Cai Jun sat down with them without a word.

The wait did not last much longer, and the glass door to the platform opened. Their guide, a smiley, thin man with few teeth, took them towards the train; they were almost on it when a chaotic stream of humans poured onto the platform and clambered over one another to get on the train. They were in the other classes and had far more luggage; people were being pushed and shoved, and small children were crying and shouting. JJ and Fred looked horrified and held their breath, almost expecting to hear an announcement of someone's death by stampede.

In the meantime, Cai Jun approached one of the train attendants and furtively pressed some money in her hand; he then urged JJ and Fred to get on the train.

Onboard, JJ and Fred discovered that their compartment was like those on the trains in France: two berths on each side, a small table in the middle. Cai Jun showed the berths assigned to them and he finally left them alone, giving them a thumbs-up as he left.

Fred immediately got comfortable on the lower berth as JJ stowed their bags.

'So, our real adventure begins!' Fred said, exhilarated.

'Alright, it looks like you have fully recovered from the fright of the crossing. I was wondering where your guts had gone.'

'Why, of course, I have always had my guts; they were just temporarily out of order.'

JJ and Fred were the first to occupy their berths, so they sat on the lower bed and watched the fascinating human flow still moving like waves towards the train. Many women had their hair cut short, while the typical style for young girls seemed to be two long braids. The men wore flat caps with a visor, similar to those worn by the communist students in France. They all seemed to don a sort of uniform in monotone colours, consisting of a couple of shades of blue, and some grey here and there. The shape of the clothes was very unbecoming for women and made them look like peasants compared to the women in Hong Kong. It did not help that some passengers still wore their winter clothing of padded jackets and padded trousers, making them look bloated.

Their survey came to an end with an arrival in their cabin: a short man with very black hair and wearing one of those blue uniforms, which looked used but clean. The man looked surprised upon seeing them and he first exclaimed something in Chinese. He sat on the bed in front of them and gazed at them openly.

Under his scrutiny, both friends turned their attention back to the window and the platform outside, which seemed to move as the train pulled out of the station. They felt the man's eyes on them and kept moving their bodies as if this would help them escape his stare. The train attendant came in and passed them a thermos; the man took one of the cups on the little table and poured hot water into it, rinsing the cup and throwing out the water directly on the floor; he then poured more hot water into the cup and started drinking the scalding liquid with obvious, painful noises. JJ and Fred looked dismayed and cringed as if they themselves had been burnt by the hot water

'Soviet?' asked the man, pointing at them with his index finger.

'No, French,' JJ replied.

'Ah, français! I lived in France for a few years. My name is Du Bo. What a coincidence that I should share the cabin with two Frenchmen. How delightful.' He had a strong accent, and he was not very fluent, but he could speak well enough to have a conversation with them.

JJ exchanged a look with Fred, who only shrugged.

'I thought you were Russian. Many of them are here in China. Our friends. We can learn from our Soviet brothers.' Du Bo told them he had spent four years in France, before the war, studying this and that. He returned to help China fight the Japanese, then he joined the Communists during the civil war. He had just finished attending a party meeting in Guangzhou on behalf of his work unit and was travelling back to Beijing, where he lived with his wife and child.

*Great*, JJ thought, *we are travelling with a Chinese party member who can speak French...*

Without having agreed on their response, JJ and Fred gave their attention to the scenery outside their window to avoid a conversation with Du Bo.

The train was travelling in slow motion through the countryside; young shoots sparkled in the blue lakes of the rice paddies; here and there farmers were bent in the fields, their trousers rolled up to the calves, their legs deep in the water, and on their heads sat conical straw hats. The paddies stretched far into the horizon, and JJ watched how the light created a gilded pattern on isolated patches of water, sometimes hitting the brown body of an ox. He wished he had his watercolours with him and frowned at the thought of the academy. Roger insisted that he should not call the academy until they reached Shanghai. But that was not the real problem. He took out the map of Shanghai to exam it.

'What are you looking for?' Fred asked.

'The harbour.' He could not do much more, as he did not have the address of Old Min's daughter with him. His stomach tensed, sending a quick rush of pain along his nerves. *One step at a time*, he reminded himself. *Now is not the time to think about Shanghai. Changsha comes first. It will all go well.*

# Chapter 21

Fred got up and left to find the toilet: just a ceramic seat with a hole in the middle. No paper, not much water, and not particularly clean. After doing his business and closing the toilet door to return to his seat, he noticed the next carriage over and decided to see what it was like. The carriage had a row of bunk beds with three levels, the topmost so high that it was not even possible to sit on it without hunching over. There were no doors and no private spaces; passengers were everywhere, on the beds, on the folding seats along one side of the carriage, some even on the floor. They were sleeping, eating, playing cards, cutting their toenails, cleaning their ears with the long nail of their pinkie… Time seemed to be suspended here as people bathed in an atmosphere of waiting, surrendering to the fact that their destinations would be a long time coming. Thus, their movements were unhurried, as if in slow motion. Only the loud voices of two or three passengers would pierce the apparent quiet of the carriage, which abruptly ceased as soon as Fred appeared.

As he walked the length of the carriage, he felt a thousand pairs of eyes on him. He quickly reached the end and turned to hurry back to his cabin, braving the stares of even more curious passengers who noticed the lǎowài's presence in the carriage.

Once in the cabin, where he found only JJ lying on the berth, Fred sat with a loud sigh. 'I have never felt so bad in my life!' he said, telling JJ about his brief excursion in the other carriage. 'I felt as if I were a German carrying a Kalashnikov and about to shoot everybody on the spot.'

'Well, we felt that in Hong Kong as well, remember?' JJ said, propping himself on his elbow to look at his friend.

'No, this is far, far worse, I tell you!'

'Oh, so you are not so enthusiastic about this trip anymore? Want to go back?' JJ said, smiling.

Fred leaned back, indifferent to JJ's teasing as well as JJ's legs trapped between the wall and his back, and said instead: 'So where is our General?'

'Do you mean the Chinese guy? I don't think he is a general.'

'Well, he was in the war. He deserves to be called General,' Fred said. 'Did you learn more about him?'

'Not much more than what he told us. I don't know where he went.'

In that moment, the General appeared at the door with three boxes and chopsticks in his hands.

'Dinner,' he said, handing a box to each of them. Du Bo looked at their surprised faces, so young and naïve, much like his own when he was in France, and his heart filled with joy. He opened his lunch box and found a large serving of white rice, thin slices of meat, and green vegetables. Du Bo felt particularly pleased to have got meat full of fat and so much rice. His mouth half full, he motioned with his chopsticks at JJ and Fred to urge them to eat.

As soon as Du Bo met the two Frenchmen, memories from his youth in France started flowing. What he remembered most was the loneliness, and the sense of being lost among people he could not understand, in a culture he was not familiar with. He often made awkward comments and sometimes he went to bed hungry because he felt overwhelmed by such simple tasks as grocery shopping or cooking.

The young men at least had each other, but Du Bo felt a moral obligation to reach out to them, and he was sure that they did not know it was possible to buy lunch boxes on the train or that they did not dare to. He had also brought a bottle of rice wine, which he poured into the large metal cups meant for tea. The more he drank, the redder his face, and the better he felt. A warmth radiated within him and around him, creating in his head a magical bond between him and the two fàguó rén.

'Life in France is for sure good. I know, I have been there,' Du Bo said proudly. 'But here in China now also very good. Under the guidance of Chairman Mao, China much better. Chairman Mao gives us a good life. Do you know Chairman Mao? Everybody loves him, everybody.' Du Bo had a radiant expression on his face.

Fred looked puzzled at JJ, who replied that he knew who Mao was.

'All is better under Chairman Mao. You see, this train too. Since its birth, China People's Republic repaired 14.0819 km of rail tracks and built 12.615 km of new tracks. Imagine that, amazing,' he said, shaking his head in disbelief.

He filled the cups up once again, indifferent to the rice wine spilling over the cups. 'Come, let's toast. To international friendship, to France and China, long live People's Republic of China, long live Chairman Mao,' Du Bo said, and he swallowed the clear liquid with a quick gulp.

With each cup, Du Bo's mind drifted away a little more and the faces of his travelling companions became more blurred. His tongue seemed to refuse to form any other French words. He tried to speak to them in

165

Mandarin, but the fàguó rén could barely recognise a word. *I could at least speak French*, he thought with superiority, forgetting all those months he could not even buy a metro ticket. *I forgot to ask why they are here*. And with this last thought, his head fell onto the table.

***

JJ was awakened by a grunting from the berth below. He leaned over to check on Fred, who got up with a jump and rushed to the door; then loud bangs were heard in the corridor. JJ looked out in time to see a Chinese lady hurrying out of the toilet and Fred hastening in. It seemed the drunken night had taken a toll on Fred's stomach.

JJ found Du Bo still sound asleep, so he took the thermos and walked down the corridor to fill it. *Hot water will make Fred feel better*, he told himself. After a while, when Fred had still not come back, JJ decided to check on him. Outside the toilet, JJ heard no noises inside, and the door was still locked. He called him, but there was no reply. He started banging on the door, to the amusement of the other passengers who had stuck their heads out of their cabins to look at the frantic lǎowài. JJ rushed back to the cabin and shook Du Bo awake.

'Du Bo, Fred is in the toilet. He is not responding, and I cannot open the door. Please help!'

Du Bo looked at JJ with drowsy eyes, not registering the words that the stranger was saying. He then slowly recovered and remembered who the stranger was and his language. He slowly got up with some effort and, unhurried, he first poured some hot water into a cup and took a sip. He grabbed two biscuits from his bag and, nibbling them, he went with JJ to check on Fred. They banged on the toilet door, but only silence followed.

Du Bo looked for a train attendant, who opened the door with a passkey. They found Fred lying on the floor, his head where one would not even like to put his feet. He had a fresh cut on his forehead. Du Bo and JJ lifted him up, and Du Bo tried to sprinkle some water on his face to wake him up. Still unconscious, Fred was carried back to the cabin. Before they reached, Du Bo stopped abruptly in the middle of the corridor, dropped his side of the motionless body, and hurried into the toilet. Ignoring JJ's cries, he threw up the two small biscuits he had just eaten, his stomach still upset by the alcohol from the night before.

Left alone, JJ dragged Fred into their cabin. He examined the cut on his friend's forehead and cleaned it with a little water as hundreds of curious eyes peeked from the doorway. JJ slapped Fred a few times on the cheek and splashed more water on his face. Fred finally came back to life.

JJ sighed. 'Finally! What is wrong with you? You scared me to death.'

Fred looked at JJ, confused. Groggy and thirsty, he took a large sip of water from the thermos, scalding his tongue. Subdued by the hangover, he laid on the berth, making a range of noises of pain.

When Du Bo entered, he looked as rumpled as Fred, minus the injury on the forehead. His eyes still dull, he sat on his berth and started apologising for making them drink so much. He inspected Fred's injury and, with a first-aid kit from the train attendant, he disinfected and bandaged the cut as best he could. Then he took a couple of trips to the restaurant car to bring three bowls of congee. The rice porridge was supposedly the best remedy against a hangover. They all ate in silence while

167

the train made yet another scheduled stop.

As JJ spooned congee into his mouth, he looked out the window at the people crowding the platform. Soon, the train was moving again, gently pulling out of the station. The passengers who had got off the train were now alone at the platform, walking to the exit. He saw a couple of families and an old lady with tiny feet. A slender man reached one small group and continued past them, in his hand was a brown-and-white chequered luggage just like their own. *How odd*, JJ thought. He expected that type of luggage to be found only in Hong Kong. He leapt from his seat, his heart beating frantically. He put his foot on the lower berth and lifted himself so he could peer into the upper berth. Stunned at what he saw, he stepped down again and shouted, 'Our luggage is gone!'

# Chapter 22

In a few hours, they would reach Changsha. For some time now, JJ's soft cry could be heard from the upper berth, accompanying the sound of the wheels rolling on the train tracks. Du Bo looked silently JJ and Fred, then turned to the scenery flittering past outside.

Nothing could have gone more wrong on this trip, and JJ blamed himself for leaving the ship with Fred, he blamed Fred for being stupid and drinking too much, and he blamed Du Bo for bringing the wine.

After a long while of unbearable silence, Du Bo spoke. 'Tell you what. I get off with you in Changsha and take you to the police station. You can report the theft. What was inside the luggage? Do you still have your documents?'

JJ held his breath for an instant, then replied, 'No.'

'Ah, that's too bad, that's too bad. Why you don't keep your documents with you? Documents are especially important. I don't know what we can do about it. You need to see the police. I am so sorry.'

*Good, at least now we have a good excuse for not having our documents with us,* thought JJ. He wondered how much money was in the bag. He had not counted it. *How stupid of me*, he thought. His mind was spinning, trying to think of solutions where there were none. *None. Why did I take this stupid trip to China? I had a perfectly nice life where I was. I had no particular needs. I did not even care about China. If I hadn't made a promise to Old Min...* Again, his stomach felt twisted.

He thought of his family, and he wished he could go back. Strangely enough, the strongest image which came to mind was that of his mother. He felt a shiver along his spine at the thought of landing in prison, or being sliced to pieces by Roger or the helmet thieves, and not seeing her again.

*Why should I care about not seeing her? Will she care if I don't go back? Are we going to prison now? If we go to the police, they will probably find out that we never went through customs. They will interrogate us, maybe torture us to make us speak.* JJ's thoughts were frantic. *What can I say? Yes, I agree I should have gone to the French Commission and not crossed the border without a passport, but my good friend here wanted too badly, and I thought it was a good idea to go with him, to show my support. You know, you cannot let friends down.* He looked at Fred, who was still sleeping off his hangover. *The money is gone. Roger will expect us to call within a few hours, to confirm we got the helmet. Oh, gosh… I want to throw up!*

\*\*\*

Du Bo was dozing in the lower berth. He wished he had a hot water bottle for his stomach pangs, which were coming in waves. He knew the pain well; it had been a relentless companion during the war, and could only be subdued with a shot of adrenaline in dangerous situations. He drank very seldom now. In the past, he often raised full glasses several times a night and with purpose. After a bottle or two, it was easier to like and be liked; the hangover the day after would become common history to be shared and laughed about many years after. This is how you built your guānxì, your network, your circle of connections that could smooth a bureaucratic matter, or grant you access to certain commodities. He was not a master at it, but it was a game everybody played. Thanks to his keen efforts to please the right people, he could get a low position in the party, which allowed him to travel a little, to earn enough, and to have a few minor privileges. But he knew he was not so smart, after all. Once, he almost risked losing his post. He had been asked to guide a small foreign delegation during a day visit in Beijing. At lunchtime, as the head of the delegation was not eating much, Du Bo kept filling his bowl. The head of the delegation, who ate out of politeness, got sick. When Du Bo tried to help him by giving him some Chinese medicine, the poor lǎowài had to be taken to the hospital. His mistake was not intentional, of course, but he had been so inept at trying to find a solution that he almost caused a diplomatic crisis. He had to thank the brother of a distant cousin who had helped him keep his job.

This time he was not personally responsible, but there was no mistake that he played a part in the misfortune of the two fàguó rén. He could hear JJ sobbing into his pillow, and he would have bitten his hand until it bled if that would have relieved him. Du Bo would take them to the police, even if he had to tell his work unit that he would be back in the office too late for a meeting. His boss would not be happy and he would have to write a critique, again. Du Bo had already written five critiques this year, and it was only May. But seeing the shock on JJ's face when he discovered the theft had hit Du Bo too strongly. So be it, he will write critique number six; he will have time on the journey from Changsha to Beijing, after leaving the fàguó rén in the hands of the police.

\*\*\*

As the train entered Changsha station, JJ was pacing in front of his cabin, glancing now and then at Fred, who still looked weak and beaten.

With no luggage to keep JJ's hands busy, he helped Fred onto the platform, followed by Du Bo. JJ let Fred go and his brow knitted at seeing how Fred wobbled his body around. This was, though, not the right time to worry about his friend. There was something bigger expecting him.

JJ had weighed all their options earlier. He most wanted to give up the deal, but then Roger would not help him with the sale of the scroll. Besides, they technically owed Roger the lost money. JJ saw but one viable option: he had to play the poker game. He needed support, though. Du Bo had looked so guilty after the theft was discovered, JJ thought, that if he'd asked him to go with them, Du Bo would agree.

'Du Bo, thank you for your help. Before going to the police, we need to meet someone. Would you come with us to help us translate?' JJ hoped that the presence of Du Bo could keep the situation from getting out of hand.

'Of course, of course,' Du Bo said eagerly.

Fred looked at his friend but shrugged as if it was none of his business, leaving JJ feeling the heavy burden of responsibility. JJ wiped away the light sweat from his hands. The next half-hour was going to decide what came next.

At the station exit, they found two men waiting for them. They were poorly dressed and clearly from the countryside. The shorter one wore a blue hat; the taller one, with a missing tooth, was wearing a white shirt that was hanging out of his blue trousers, clearly clothes that had been worn for a few days already. Du Bo could smell the stench. *How are these two peasants connected to the fàguó rén?* Du Bo registered the surprise of the two strangers at seeing him with the lǎowài.

He approached them with a friendly face and said, 'Bad news. The young men here had their luggage stolen. They have to report the theft to the police, but I can go with them. I feel sort of responsible for what happened.'

The two men looked at each other, confused, slowly grasping what he was saying.

'They have no money?' they asked Du Bo.

'Yes, yes, they have money, but the luggage and their passports are gone,' replied Du Bo, thinking about the small amount of cash he knew the two friends still had on them.

The two men nodded and started walking towards a nearby hotel. Du Bo kept insisting that they go to the police station, but seeing that JJ and Fred were following the other men, he went with them, not understanding what was happening.

Once in a room, Du Bo found himself in the interpreter's role and half-willingly helped JJ and the two men communicate, while Fred threw himself on the small leather couch in a corner.

'Where is the money?' asked the tall man.

JJ took out a small roll of bills and put it on the table where they were all seated.

The two men pointed at the money. 'What is this? This is not what we agreed on,' one said, uncertain.

The man with the blue cap took the roll and started counting, finishing much sooner that JJ wished. 'This is joke. This is not even enough to pay for a jade bracelet.'

Du Bo translated and JJ answered he did not know what they meant; he was just a courier, and he had been told to meet them and give them that money to get a helmet or something similar from them.

'Fuck, the foreigners want to cheat us.' The toothless man jumped to his feet and shouted loudly, looking at Du Bo. 'Tell them they cannot cheat us.'

JJ replied before letting Du Bo speak. 'I know nothing. Tell them we don't know. We are two students who agreed to bring the money here in exchange for a little pocket money for us.'

'You're lying. We agreed on a much higher price,' the toothless man said. 'We know Cai Jun. He would never cheat us. You are the one cheating.'

'Here,' JJ said, sacrificing the last two banknotes he had planned to keep for the rest of the journey. 'Take these too. This is really all we have. No more money, nothing.'

The men kept shouting, took the helmet out, and showed it to them.

Immediately, several pairs of eyes turned to the small rigid cap, whose bright white colour contrasted with the dark table. Its shape recalled the hairstyle of the ancient Egyptian statues JJ often saw at the Louvre.

'Look, look, it is all jade, every single piece. This is worth much more than that. For that money, we cannot sell. The helmet is worth several jade bracelets!'

JJ also got up and started raising his voice. 'You don't want to sell, don't sell. I don't care. Give me the money back and let's end it here. We have to go to the police to report the theft of our passports.'

Du Bo struggled to keep up with the pace of the conversation in both languages, but he understood that something dubious was going on and was eager to leave to go to the police station.

'I'm a party member. I don't know what's going on, but I don't support it. Remember that he who harms the people will not easily escape justice,' Du Bo said.

The two men were taken aback and looked at each other nervously.

'What do you have there? How much are your watches worth?' one of them asked, nodding towards JJ and then Fred, who had fallen asleep.

JJ took off his watch and Fred's, who woke but did not react, and put them both on the table. 'Take these too. That's all. You now either take them or let us go.'

The door opened and a middle-aged woman stood at the entrance: 'My name is Yan Caofang. Cai Jun sent me to pick up two foreigners,' she said.

JJ saw a scared look on the face of the two men; they quickly grabbed the money and the watches, and left the helmet as they rushed to leave. The tall one turned and said, 'You watch out, lǎowài. We will tell Cai Jun that you cheated us. You will pay the consequences.'

With that, they left JJ, Fred, and the two perplexed Chinese staring at one another. Fred was now fully awake, and JJ reached out for the glass of hot water that a waitress had served when they first entered the room. With shaking hands, he took a sip, then ran his hands over his face several times.

'I think you owe me some explanations,' Du Bo said, holding the jade helmet in his hands.

JJ closed his eyes for a moment. He had no more energy to make up another story; he had already told too many lies in the last three days. He was still incredulous that he had been able to pull off this last act. As the adrenaline abated, he told Du Bo the entire story, glad to unburden himself. This was his last gamble: convincing Du Bo to let them go.

'So, here it is. This is the helmet. If we go to the police, we will be in trouble. I did not want to do anything bad. I just wanted to reach Shanghai in time to keep a promise to my old teacher,' JJ finished.

'But I should take you to the police. This is state property. Even if you did not steal it, you cannot keep it.'

'We are not keeping it. Our friend is selling it to someone in Shanghai.'

'What? This is highly illegal too. Who is this person?'

'We don't know, but I guess someone very wealthy.'

Du Bo picked up the helmet and wrapped it again carefully; he had to think. The young men had made a mistake, but they were simple middlemen who had nothing to gain, really, from the situation, except getting to Shanghai. If Du Bo went to the police, the two would get arrested and who knows what was going to happen to them. Their lives would be ruined because of a youthful mistake; even if they came out of prison, they would not be the same again.

Du Bo had himself spent time in prison. He had been captured with a few others by the Nationalists during a guerrilla action and imprisoned for several months before his comrades somehow succeeded in getting him out with a mix of bribery and violence. He had a cause he was fighting for, but still found the prison conditions bad enough. Going to jail for being young and unexperienced would be even more unbearable, he thought. They could be his sons. Back home, they have parents who would never see them again, maybe. For one mistake. There was no other choice to make, was there?

# Chapter 23

Du Bo thanked Caofang for her invitation to spend the night at her place together with JJ and Fred. Once in the flat, she left for work. Du Bo placed the helmet on the table and inspected it from all sides. He sat rubbing his face with his hands several times, flustered. One hour passed, and Du Bo was still sitting and looking at the helmet, not speaking a word. JJ and Fred watched from another room, where they could smoke and stay out of sight as they waited for what seemed like a verdict. Time was suspended, as it had been during the border crossing. Would they come under fire again? Would they get hit this time?

Du Bo got up and waved JJ and Fred into the room. 'We are all together in this,' he said. 'I risk my job and more, and you also risk going to jail. This is how I see the situation, and we either do it my way or I go to the police.' The choices were loud and clear: either turn themselves in to the police or defy Roger.

So, JJ and Fred agreed with Du Bo on a deal, one that could lead them to freedom or to jail.

*** 

Compared to Guangzhou's train station, Changsha's was much smaller but still overflowing with people. JJ looked around to locate a phone to call Yvette.

She answered after one ring. 'Your friend left a few hours ago. Yesterday he had a quarrel with the Chinese friend. They spoke about money... '

'Yvette, you were eavesdropping?' said JJ, cracking a little smile. He could sense from her silence that she was embarrassed.

'No, not on purpose. They were louder than the usual 'Chinese' loud.' She whispered, turning her back to the maid and looking at the door to make sure she was not overheard. 'I found the article.'

JJ did not know what she was talking about.

'The article about the theft of a helmet. Are you involved in this, JJ?'

JJ took a deep breath. So, this was what Father Kurt knew. 'We did not steal it,' he said, not feeling as bad for telling her a half-truth.

'I know you didn't. They stole it months before you arrived in China.'

JJ fiddled with the phone cord, then asked Yvette what her husband's intentions were.

'I didn't tell him. But he spent quite some time talking to Roger before he left.'

JJ was baffled. 'What did you mean, that he knows what we did, then?'

'The passports, you crossed the border illegally, of course. You are not spies, are you?'

Against his will, JJ laughed out loud. He thought how pleased Fred would be to be thought of as a spy. JJ told Yvette briefly the story and the turn of events up to that point.

'And now?' she asked.

'Now we are heading to Shanghai and we will sell the helmet,' JJ said.

Yvette remained silent again, and JJ imagined her serious expression, her serious brown eyes, which only gleamed with the occasional laugh, and her calm manners.

'Don't… don't forget that you have a friend here. If

you need anything, let me know,' Yvette said softly.

'Thanks.' He then heard himself blurt out, 'Can you call my parents?' *What the hell am I saying? Call them to say what?*

Again, his voice was speaking against his will. 'Tell them I love them, I love my mother and apologise for… ' He did not know what he should apologise for, but he thought that in a goodbye message, one should be contrite. Should he apologise for being born?

*How silly am I*, he thought. *Why am I thinking about goodbyes? It is going to be okay. Somehow this absurd story will finish and I will get on with my life and my plan to find Old Min's daughter, sell the scroll, and go home…*

'Yes, give me the number,' she urged.

'No, forget it. I am talking rubbish. All is fine, no need to call them. They probably don't remember me anyway,' he joked.

'Tell me the number, anyway.'

He gave her the number.

'Can you call me once you arrive in Shanghai?' Yvette asked.

JJ agreed and hung up. Somewhere along this journey, Yvette had become his voice of reason, thanks to her pragmatic and simple ways.


Meanwhile, Du Bo had found another phone to call his wife. Earlier, he had had trouble buying a ticket and had to stress his position in the party to get one. He asked himself why he was risking so much; after all, he was no longer a young idealist who thought he could change the world.

Even his wife sounded concerned on the phone. The political atmosphere had been tense recently: a couple of long-standing party supporters had been accused of

179

acting against the party. He knew that if he made a mistake with his plan, his family would also pay the consequences. His position in the administration was already precarious, as his boss had long wanted to get rid of him. Now Du Bo had the chance to accomplish something that would put him in such a good light that his boss would not be able to touch him. Maybe he would even be offered a position in another unit. He could then breathe and stop fearing that every day at work could be his last.

***

The train arrived in Shanghai after a long and uneventful trip, the three of them occupying three sleepers in two compartments. JJ seemed to be in a bad mood the whole time. He periodically found himself raising his arm to check the time, only to remember he had sold his watch.

Fred was in a foul temper as well. 'That was unfair. You took advantage of me and gave them my watch without my consent,' he complained for the fifth or sixth time.

'Why did you have to drink so much?' JJ said. 'It was a mess. I had no choice. Now we are stuck with Du Bo. What if he changes his mind and takes us to the police?'

Fred was annoyed with JJ and his air of superiority. He might like to live the life of a nun, looking at nature and staying in his own corner, but Fred was a man, and to him, there nothing wrong with drinking a little. 'What, you never drank yourself? Why did you not let me be?' Fred said, raising his voice. 'I was just a little sick. It happens when you drink. What's the big deal?'

'This is a whole other thing—much worse than just missing the ship. We now have even more chance to land in jail,' JJ said, speaking fast.

'Why did you not think about it before then? I did not force you to come with me,' Fred said, putting both hands on his hips.

'I did not want to let you go alone.'

'Bullshit, you came because you worried about the ashes of your teacher. If you could have had a passport in one day, you would already be in Shanghai,' Fred said with a challenge in his eye, which JJ left unmet.

***

At the Shanghai train station, JJ tried to reach Roger. The call went unanswered again. Du Bo suggested to first find an accommodation and took them to the old town.

JJ saw Fred was ready to speak, and he hurried to agree, as behind Du Bo's back he signalled Fred not to add a word.

Du Bo led the way, while JJ and Fred followed a few steps behind.

'Why did you agree? It would be easier to just stay in the hotel Marcel is in. We get our passport back, and a proper room to sleep,' Fred said, then added with hope, 'and a real bathroom, and fresh clothing.'

'You forgot we must avoid reporting to the police, remember? Du Bo knows better, how we can do that.'

At the reception desk of a hotel Du Bo knew was cheap and clean, he pretended to have just met the foreigners on the train to Shanghai and was helping them find a room. The receptionist, a middle-aged woman with a birthmark on one cheek, started a discussion with Du Bo, which JJ and Fred could not follow. At a certain point, they saw Du Bo take his luggage and usher them to the door.

'They don't accept guests without passports. Don't worry. We try another one,' he said, his voice still firm and sure.

They walked to the next one, a building close to a pile of rubbish. Without Du Bo, JJ and Fred would have never ventured there.

Another conversation at the reception desk with, this time, a man who, despite the cool evening, wore a jacket open at his chest, showing his white undershirt and an enormous belly. JJ also noticed his face was red from drinking. The man appeared more friendly than the woman, but he also refused to give them a room. This time, Du Bo's voice was less steady when he urged them to move on and look somewhere else.

They went back to a somewhat larger street. Sticking out of the wood-framed windows of low-rise buildings were poles hanging laundry. JJ and Fred also noted the red banners fluttering in the light breeze. Multiple cables were fixed hazardously, either on the front buildings or on the roofs. Shops took up the ground floor and sold various objects, from shining pots in all sizes, to brushes, ink and paper, to shoes and clothing. The alleys were busy with people, some sitting, others standing outside or eating rice from bowls. The atmosphere was similar to that of Hong Kong streets, even if somewhat shabbier. The Frenchmen were, of course, the attraction of the day, and some curious children even dared come closer to shout something at them.

Du Bo didn't know where to look next for an accommodation when he spotted a vendor selling bāozi. His stomach growled at the thought of eating a Chinese bun, and he bought a few. He handed one bāozi filled with meat to JJ and another to Fred.

'Eat,' he encouraged them.

All three men stood in front of the stall, eating their warm buns. Du Bo started a conversation with the vendor, appraising him quietly: his eyes were keen, his bāozi excellent. *This guy really knows his trade*, Du Bo thought.

'Tóngzhì, comrade, do you know where I can find accommodation for them?' Du Bo asked. 'They are a little lost and have not much money.'

The man heard the question but hesitated to answer.

Du Bo faked a little laugh. 'I know, I know, hard to believe. But they are studying in Hangzhou, they told me. They skipped a class and took a train to visit the big city. They have heard so much about the Bund and the beauties of Shanghai.'

The vendor looked absorbed with his work, placing a spoonful of filling on a piece of flattened dough, then wrapping it into the bāozi form. Du Bo noticed his eyes flicking between him and the two fàguó rén.

'You could try the hostel of Madame Sun. It is not far,' the vendor finally said. He gave terse instructions to Du Bo, who thanked him and paid for the bāozi, adding a little extra for the helpful tip.

Madame Sun's place was hard to locate, and when Du Bo realised they were going around in circles, he asked for directions. Two passers-by did not seem to know, but when Du Bo asked a third person, a young woman in a traditional qipao overheard him.

'Dà yè, uncle, are you looking for Madame Sun? I can take you there. I know the way.'

Du Bo was a little taken aback by the appearance of the woman with the tiniest smile, who was examining the foreigners from the corners of her eyes. Du Bo agreed to follow her. She could speak some broken English, and a suspicion popped up in Du Bo's mind.

After a while, they stopped in front of a well-maintained building. Flowers decorated the entrance and the windows above, in a marked difference from the surrounding houses, most of which were in awful shape. There was no reception desk as such but rather a few traditional chairs, which were of modest value but had obviously been recently polished. On the wall, there were elegant drawings of half-naked courtesans, and Du Bo felt embarrassed to see his suspicions confirmed. Their guide shouted and Madame Sun came out from a side room. The woman explained on their behalf that the three men wanted a room for the night.

JJ stared with admiration at Madame Sun's embroidered silk dress. He estimated the lady, who for sure had been a beauty in her youth, was now in her sixties. She was heavily perfumed, her clothing was neat without being expensive, and her hair and make-up were skilfully done, somewhat similar to those of the woman who brought them here. Madame Sun's figure was much fuller, though, and she seemed to have difficulties moving around.

Madame Sun's piercing eyes appraised JJ and Fred.

'Where are you from?' she asked in English.

'We are French,' JJ replied. He hinted a smile, but it soon died on his lips when the lady did not react to his friendly tone. She was standing still, her face impassive, as if emotions never touched her.

JJ gave a side glance to Fred, as he heard Madame Sun speaking again, this time in passable French.

'You want to spend the night here?'

'Yes, we have had a long journey and we need a room for the night,' Fred said, speaking for the first time since the quarrel in the train.

'You want to spend the night here, three men in a room?'

This time JJ, Fred, and Du Bo looked at each another, as if confirming silently that they all agreed to share a room.

Madame Sun smirked. She told them in Chinese the price of the room.

'Nàme guì! It cannot be so expensive,' Du Bo said, taking over the conversation.

'You want the room the whole night. There will be one room less available for my business; You cover for the missed opportunity. You take it or not, it is not my problem. You need help, I can offer you a room at that price, no questions asked,' she explained, her hoarse voice betraying a habit of heavy smoking. 'You share a room. I cannot give you two. I'll ask a girl to take you there. The bathroom is communal, at the end of corridor.'

With that, she stretched her hand out, clearly expecting that they would take her offer.

Reluctantly, Du Bo paid for the room, the corners of his tight lips turned down.

# Chapter 24

A young maid led the men up the staircase to a large room. She handed them three towels and a bar of soap, then left an ewer of lukewarm water next to a basin on a tripod. There was only one large bed in the room. Despite the prospect of having to share the bed, JJ was relieved that Du Bo had found them a place to stay and had solved at least one problem. The next one was to find a phone that could call international, which had been difficult in Changsha, where only a couple of five-star hotels had such a line.

Luckily, they were not too far from the famous Bund, where Du Bo told JJ they could for sure find a hotel from which to call Hong Kong. They left the room and walked towards the embankment, which was occupied by grand colonial buildings erected at the beginning of the century by several countries. The sheer length and space of the Bund usually mesmerised visitors, and while Fred was awestruck, JJ, due to his regular visits to the majestic Avenue des Champs-Élysées, appreciated the view without being too impressed.

Despite the late hour, the Huangpu River was still full of life, with shimmering light coming off the sampans transporting goods. It was past ten and several kilometres later, when they found one at Broadway Mansions, at the far end of the Bund.

JJ dialled Roger's number, and this time, he picked up immediately.

'Damn you, why did you take so long?' Roger yelled from the other end. JJ had only murmured a short hello before Roger erupted.

'I have been waiting for your call! What happened?' he said, as if he were commanding coolies at the tin mine back in Malaysia.

'There have been some problems, but all is fine. We have the helmet,' JJ replied.

'What problems?'

'We could not find a phone. They sent us to the wrong place, and we almost missed the train,' JJ lied, as Fred and Du Bo sat next to him tensely. His forehead was sweating while he talked. He was surprised at the amount of lies he had told, as well as the amount of sweat on his body had produced since being in China.

'How can we contact the buyer? We want to hand this over as soon as possible,' JJ said.

'Well, damn you. It is after ten pm. I cannot call the buyer at this time to arrange the meeting.'

'Roger, why don't you give me the name and telephone number. We can call him directly. Isn't that easier?' suggested JJ, giving Du Bo a look, not that Du Bo could understand the conversation in English, anyway.

'And how would you speak with him? He cannot speak English.'

*Okay*, JJ thought. This was a small clue: the buyer was not someone who regularly associated with foreigners. Did it mean something, though? *On the contrary, it widens the possibilities.*

'You have to call me back tomorrow, at this other phone number. It is my office's. Do not leave a message with anyone. Ask for me and say that you are calling for the discounted goods I offered.'

JJ hung up and looked at Du Bo, shaking his head. 'Sorry, he did not give any information this time. We have to call back tomorrow.'

Du Bo tightened his lips. 'Too bad, too bad. We need to be fast. I need to go back to Beijing, money for stay is not much, Shanghai is expensive.'

The long walk back to Madame Sun's took all their energy and once in bed, they fell asleep immediately, laying close side by side as if they were a family.

*** 

JJ was the first to wake up the next morning. 'Fred, get up, come on. We are going to the hotel to find your brother.'

Fred stretched in bed and groaned.

Du Bo headed to the toilet first, leaving the two friends in the room. Their argument on the train had left tension between them, and they had since been cautious around each other.

'Say, why do we still have to deliver the helmet? Du Bo could do it alone,' Fred said.

JJ turned to Fred so fast, he heard a crack in his neck. 'We cannot leave him alone to do it. He might get into trouble. And we have to get the money to Roger as well.'

'Well, nobody asked Du Bo to get mixed up with the deal. What can Roger do to us now if we don't sell it?'

JJ looked at Fred, who was propped up on his side with his head in his hand and elbow on the bed, and his ankles crossed over.

'What are you saying? You want to break your promises, both to Roger and Du Bo? And what the hell do you want to do with the helmet?'

'Relax, JJ, you are always so uptight. All I am saying is that we are here in Shanghai and our problems are now solved. I think that if Roger or Du Bo still want our cooperation, we should get paid for it.'

'We have an agreement with both.'

'So what? Agreements can be broken if situations change. We have the strongest position now. All I'm saying is we should take advantage of that,' Fred said, scratching his chest.

'You cannot break a promise,' JJ said.

'Look who's talking… Didn't you break your promise not to wander alone in the garden back in Phnom Penh? And didn't you also break your promise to your teacher, to hand over his ashes to his daughter?' Fred said, getting up. He shot a disdainful glance at JJ and opened the door, saying, 'Stop lecturing me. You are not without faults.'

Moments later, Du Bo entered the room and found JJ motionless near the window, his face as white as a mourning sheet.

'Aiya, what is it with you, my friend? You look sick, was it the food yesterday?'

As no answer or reaction came, Du Bo reached for JJ's pulse and asked to show him his tongue.

At this, JJ came to his senses and focused his eyes on Du Bo. 'I am fine,' he said.

'You don't look fine.' Du Bo placed three fingers on JJ's pulse. 'Show me your tongue.'

JJ looked at him with a grimace. 'Why should I show you my tongue, for heaven's sake?'

'It's Chinese medicine. I can see what is wrong with you.'

'Ce n'est rien. It's nothing. I just had a few words with Fred.' He sat on the bed to put his socks on.

'Ah, you quarrelled. It happens, but friends are friends.'

JJ paused, his hands still on one of his socks. 'He…
he is different from what I thought.'

The tone of his voice made Du Bo turn to face JJ; he
went to sit next to him. 'What is better? To not trust a
friend or to be betrayed by a friend? In China we say
better trust.' Du Bo patted him on his leg and went to
finish dressing.

*What if, by trusting a friend, I betray two others?* JJ
asked himself silently.

***

At Marcel's hotel, the reception was immaculately
clean and quiet, but not as sumptuous as the Broadway
Mansions, from which they had called Roger. They
approached the desk, and Du Bo asked for Marcel
Marechal. The receptionist took the guest register and
checked the names, then she came back.

'Sorry, I don't see any guests with this name.'

Du Bo asked Fred whether he was sure this was the
hotel.

'Yes, of course. I read the travel documents a hundred
times. I am sure of it. How many Friendship Hotels are
there in the city?'

'Only one, one in Shanghai, and one in each major
Chinese city,' laughed Du Bo, while Fred looked
annoyed at the receptionist. 'Please check again. My
friend is sure that his brother is here.'

'How do you write the name?'

Fred took a pen and wrote the name on a piece of
paper, which the receptionist took with a smile. She had
to squint to read Fred's handwriting and went to the
register again.

'Oh, yes. Here is his name.'

Du Bo turned to Fred and JJ. 'She found him.'

Fred and JJ relaxed and smiled.

'他离开了,' she said to Du Bo.

For a moment, the miniature waterfall was the only sound in the reception hall. Then the receptionist and Du Bo went back and forth.

'怎么了? 不可能吧。请你再查一下。'

'他是跟 一个贸易代表团过来的, 对吧?'

'是的，是的。'

'我知道了。他好像去香港了。我们帮他买一张票，他住了两个晚上就走了。'

Du Bo turned to the two friends.

'Ton frère… your brother, he stayed here for two nights and then left for Hong Kong. He is not here.'

'He left? With all my luggage? And passport?' JJ asked, his voice resounding in the lobby.

Du Bo asked the lady.

'It seems so. The lady says he had lots of luggage for one person only,' Du Bo said.

JJ closed his eyes, and when he opened them, they were full of unshed tears.

Fred kept swearing to himself, hitting the reception desk with his fist.

Du Bo asked the receptionist whether it was possible to make a call to Hong Kong from the hotel.

'Only from the guest rooms, sorry.'

'Allons-y, les enfants… let's go. We have to call your friend in Hong Kong,' Du Bo said, taking JJ and Fred by the arm to lead them outside.

They walked toward the Bund and to the same hotel from last night. Du Bo noticed that spring had brought colour to the street, and he pointed to some large trees decorating one of the main alleys. 'Look, these are tilias.

Their smell is so strong that they spread their scent along the whole street. Too bad it is not their season yet.'

'Do you really think we care about trees?' Fred said, showing his teeth as if wanting to bite into something.

'I know, I know. Zhēn máfan, very troublesome. Let's first settle the call with your friend, then we can discuss?' Du Bo said.

'You only care about your damned helmet. We are stuck here again, with no passports and no money,' Fred shouted. With a red face, he quickened his pace to walk ahead of JJ and Du Bo.

'What do you think, JJ? What are your options?' Du Bo asked.

'I don't think anything. I don't know. It is clear that we must return to Hong Kong. At least, I must go to Hong Kong. I need my luggage back. I have something important in there.' A thought flashed in his mind. 'Mon Dieu, I hope Marcel did not travel all the way back to France.'

'That would be very inconvenient indeed.'

JJ did not listen to him. 'I would have to go back to France to get Old Min's ashes back.' He moaned and fell to his knees, holding his belly.

'What is it? Stomach pains? I told you, it was probably the food. You show me no tongue, is okay. I take you to drink herbal tea, good for your stomach.'

JJ looked at him, completely lost.

# Chapter 25

Back at his office, Roger waited for a call from JJ, which arrived shortly after two pm. He told JJ the meeting would take place in Hangzhou.

'Why do we have to go to Hangzhou if he lives in Shanghai? You know that without a passport and with our little Chinese, getting train tickets is difficult for us,' JJ replied.

Roger could hear the distress in his voice. 'Shit, I did not think about it,' he said, adding, 'But Fred's brother is in Shanghai. Didn't you get your passports?'

'We went to the hotel, but apparently he has gone back to Hong Kong,' JJ said. Each time he thought about or pronounced the words 'Hong Kong', his stomach contracted.

'That's troublesome. I must call the buyer back and see if we can do the deal in Shanghai. Do you have a phone number where I can reach you?'

JJ gave him the phone number at Madame Sun's. 'That would still not solve our problem though,' JJ said.

'Well, you wanted to go to China.'

'Yes, I know but I need to get my luggage back, and my passport. How can we reach Hong Kong from here?'

'Kid, without passports, you know that there is only one way out.'

'Cross the border illegally again,' JJ said in a flat tone.

'Yes. But I don't know if I can help you this time,' Roger said.

JJ hung up and told his two companions about Roger's instructions. Then the three men spent the rest of the day in the room waiting for Roger to call.

Du Bo frowned as he read a newspaper that he had found on the street. He wanted to go home as soon as possible. They were running out of money and he felt the situation was getting too complicated. He could not help the fàguó rén with their missing passports, and it was as dangerous to have further contact with them after the deal.

JJ had popped out for some food at a nearby stall, but his presence was attracting a lot of attention and several passers-by had stopped to observe him as he ate or comment with other onlookers. JJ did not like it, but he was much less bothered, as his mind was occupied with bigger concerns. He concentrated on slurping up a long string of noodle without scalding his mouth with the soup. He took a second bite.

After finishing, he walked back toward the Bund, where he felt the spacious waterfront allowed him to breathe. Alone and with his back to the passing crowd, he felt less conspicuous, and he enjoyed some moments of solitude. Leaning towards the water, he observed life on the Huangpu River, where there was an array of junks similar to the one they had taken to cross into China. The river was wide and the other side seemed devoid of all life, only a few low construction sites were visible among an expanse of uncultivated fields. He realised that since he had boarded the ship in Marseille, he had never really been alone. Fred had been his companion since JJ first opened the door of the cabin. He felt drained of all his energy, and he admitted to himself that he was also dreading what would come next.

*** 

In the quiet hall of Madame Sun's lodgings, the phone rang. After three rings, a maid picked up and listened to someone speaking Cantonese. Not understanding, she passed the receiver to Madame Sun, who immediately recognised a Western accent and replied in English. After a brief conversation, she knew the call was for the guests upstairs and sent the maid to fetch the men.

Fred came down to take the call, but as he could not really understand, he asked Madame Sun to help. She listened and then wrote the address in English as well as in Chinese and gave it to Fred. He went back upstairs with a sense of victory, as if he had won a prize, and announced to Du Bo that he had everything they needed: tomorrow was going to be the day.

'What's his name?' Du Bo asked.

'Whose name? Roger?'

'No, the name of the buyer.'

Fred looked at the piece of paper and said, 'I don't know. It is not written here.'

'What? He didn't tell you the name?' Du Bo asked, 'You didn't ask for the name?' He repeated the question, thinking that he was too agitated for his French to be understood.

'I don't know. No, I didn't. The conversation was too fast.'

'You have no name! But this is what we need! No name, no plan. But then also no help for you!' Du Bo said, his anger rising. He took a deep breath and tried to calm down.

'Repeat what he told you,' Du Bo demanded.

'I don't know! I don't know! Madame Sun talked to him. I could not understand him well enough.'

Du Bo inhaled deeply and went downstairs to Madame Sun, hoping to get more information. He had a hard frown on his face and a powerful urge to slap the boy.

*** 

Tired of walking, JJ sat on a low wall enclosing the flower beds of the Bund, near to a middle-aged man performing slow, meditative movements. The man was practising with such an intense focus that he seemed oblivious to his surroundings, thus JJ could observe him at ease. The old man's movements, enchained one after the other, created a harmonious flow, which emanated peace and harmony. JJ thought he could picture Yvette doing the same exercises with the same calm expression. He felt a longing, unfamiliar to him, to share his trouble with someone. He decided he had to make two calls.

He got up and walked again towards the Broadway Mansions. In its lobby, JJ stood in a phone booth. He heard the phone ring a few times before Yvette picked up.

'JJ, so glad to hear from you. Have you arrived safely in Shanghai?'

'Yes, but… it's a mess.' He told her a short version of the story.

Yvette listened quietly, jolts of adrenaline reaching her hands so that they grasped the receiver even tighter.

'We need to settle our situation with the helmet and Roger. I also need to collect something in Hangzhou.' He had not told Yvette about the scroll yet. 'According to Du Bo's plan, we are supposed to give the helmet to the buyer, take the money, and then disappear; but the problem now is, how can we disappear without our passports?'

'JJ, go to the police and report the theft of the passports.'

'I can't do that now. Du Bo might get into trouble if they somehow make a connection between him and us.' JJ also worried about how he could explain the delay in reporting the theft.

'Then come back to Guangzhou. We will go to the police here; we will say that you stayed with us all this time. We will take care of it.' Yvette heard an indistinct wheeze on the other end; she could not tell whether it was a sigh of relief or a cry. 'These are not the best times for foreigners in China, but we still enjoy some respect from the authorities.'

'What will your husband say?' *Or do*, JJ added in his head.

'Nothing. He was disappointed when I told him I could find nothing in the papers. He seemed to have dropped the subject,' Yvette said. 'Shall I call your mother?' she then offered.

JJ hesitated. 'No, I will call her.'

After he said goodbye to Yvette, he slowly punched in another number on the telephone's rotary dial, his fingers trembling.

A woman's voice replied, crisp and clear.

'Allô, Mamam? It's me,' JJ said.

There was a scream on the other side. 'Where are you? We are worried sick! We received a call from the school saying that you did not show up. Are you okay?'

JJ was stunned at the reaction. 'I did not think you would worry. Sorry,' he said, thinking his mother was being dramatic.

'Of course, I'm worried. I know you are a brave and sensible young man. I can trust you to travel all the way there alone. But when I did not hear from you, I imagined the worst. Are you still in Hong Kong then? I am so relieved to hear you are okay. I was already looking for passage to China,' his mother said, without taking a single break between each word.

Wondering why his mother felt the need to pretend, he said, 'No, I am in China and—'

His mother cut him short. 'How did you get to China? Your father contacted the captain, and he said that you were reported missing when the ship left Hong Kong. What happened?'

JJ was taken aback at his mother's words. Did they really go as far as talking to the captain? 'It's a long story,' he said, and he gave his mother the minimum amount of information to secure her help.

'Oh, mon chéri, why did you do that?' Her slight reproaching tone was more familiar to him.

'I was helping a friend, Maman.'

'Oh, my child, what kind of friend wants you to do something illegal? You should have called us immediately after missing the boat. What would your father say now? He was anxious and started asking around in Hong Kong, to no avail. He will get mad, I can assure you.'

JJ replied with a silence.

'What can I tell your father? He has already accused me of being a horrible mother to let you leave. Of course, he forgot he was the one who agreed in the first place to let you go. Short memory as always, the fault always lies with others. I will first write him a letter to explain and ask for help.'

'Why write a letter?' JJ asked, suddenly alert. 'Is he travelling?'

198

His mother hesitated. 'We are taking a break. Well, no, I am taking a break, maybe a longer one. You see, mon Jeanou, we do not really understand each other anymore, me and your father. He does not like my hair, he does not like that I study, that I work. He wants me to be like the ornaments around the flat, beautiful and silent. But I am a person, and I have a right to live. I cannot do only what he wants, n'est-ce pas?'

JJ could hear from the flow of words and its speed how upset his mother was. 'Are you and Father finally getting a divorce?'

His mother fell silent. 'Well, I don't know. Your father does not agree, so I suppose we must be separated two years before requesting one. But we love you, JJ, and this has nothing to do with you.'

'Yes, sure,' he said, his voice flat.

'I will try to contact your father. How can I reach you?'

'I will call you back. But first I need an urgent favour.'

His mother listened closely and told him she would find a solution. Despite her reassurance, moments later, he hung up with mixed feelings.

***

Back at Madame Sun's, JJ found Fred and Du Bo in their room. Their Chinese companion looked agitated.

'Where you were?' Du Bo asked. 'We have no name! Why did you leave us alone? You know your friend here not speak English, your contact called, and he did not understand a thing. We have no name! We have nothing! I risk for nothing, no name. I am just a stupid who not show up at work.'

JJ needed a moment to understand what had happened. 'You are so right, Du Bo. I must apologise for my stupidity. I have been making one mistake after the other. I don't know what to do,' JJ said sadly. He threw himself on the bed and rubbed his tired eyes.

'My friend, I see this; you call your friend talk to him, yes? Tell him give you name? How you be sure you give object to right person?' Du Bo's French had deteriorated during the day, and by this time, his accent was thicker. His voice was full of urgency and worry. 'You maybe find way to go out China but me, nothing in hands.'

Without opening his eyes, JJ replied in a soft voice, 'We would need to get out again to call. I've walked for so long already,' he said, his exhausted limbs heavy on the bed. He felt himself sink into sleep.

# Chapter 26

JJ felt a mild tap on his hand and waved in the air to get rid of what he thought was a fly. The tapping started again, this time a tiny voice calling his name followed the touch. He opened his eyes and saw Du Bo looking at him from a close distance.

A light knock. JJ stirred a little as Du Bo went to open the door.

'A call for you,' a maid said.

They all jumped to their feet; JJ hurried downstairs, followed by Du Bo, while Fred remained in the room, unconcerned.

'Where were you? I called before,' JJ heard Roger say as soon as he picked up the waiting receiver.

'I know, sorry. I was out taking some fresh air. We are so glad you called back.'

'Of course, I called back. Did you expect me to give the important information to a Chinese stranger? How did you get a room, by the way, without documents?' Roger asked.

'We are in a whorehouse,' JJ said outright. *Better to tell the truth and avoid further questions*, he thought.

Roger laughed. 'I knew you were resourceful. My respect!'

'But it's expensive here. We almost have no money left.'

'Okay, don't worry. Tomorrow you will earn some money to cover your expenses. Now, the buyer is a certain Ning Fu. Sorry, but he insisted on meeting you in Hangzhou. At the Friendship Hotel in Hangzhou.

Take a bus; they do not check any documents for bus rides. He will meet you in the lobby and take you to a guest room. Now listen carefully: from there he will call me, and we close the deal on the spot. You must count the money. We agreed on a price of 400,000 yuan. Make sure it's all there before giving him the helmet.'

JJ held his breath. They had a name.

'Ning Fu,' JJ said, repeating the name for the benefit of Du Bo, whose blood was coming back to his pale face.

Roger continued, 'Once the deal is all done, you go to the train station and give the money to Cai Jun; he will come from Guangzhou to pick it up. No need to pay me back the money I lent you.'

'Do you think we can travel back to Guangzhou with him?' JJ asked.

'No, I am sorry. He finds it too risky to travel by car with you. You are on your own,' Roger said.

'But did you not say you were going to help me sell the scroll, after the deal?' JJ asked, frantic.

'Sure. When you make it back to Hong Kong, call me.' And with that, he hung up.

JJ sighed. Although he knew that Roger only cared about the sale of the helmet, the Dutchman's dismissal still disappointed him.

*\*\**

Fred heard steps approaching, and he hurried to get in bed and close his eyes, unwilling to speak to JJ.

The door opened and JJ and Du Bo entered the room. Fred could not say whether or not the call was good news, as his travel companions were both silent. His curiosity got the better of him, and he opened his eyes.

Without a word, he caught JJ's look.

'It was Roger. We have a name. We are travelling tomorrow to Hangzhou to sell the helmet.' JJ sat on the bed and started undressing, while he told Fred about his call with Yvette and her suggestion.

'Back to Guangzhou? But I don't want to go to the pol—' Fred did not like the sound of Yvette's idea, but JJ interrupted him.

'Fred, I don't care. Do what you want. I'm going to Guangzhou and will report the loss of my passport. You can stay here and find a solution for yourself.'

Fred pursed his lips as if he had just swallowed a lemon. 'Well, I'll agree to go to Guangzhou with you, but I won't go to the police. I will ask Roger to help me cross the border again.'

'Whatever,' JJ replied, rolling his eyes.

'Quiet, quiet,' Du Bo urged them, sitting up on the bed. 'Let's sleep now, tomorrow, big day.' His earlier attempts to bring peace between the two friends had floundered, like drops of rain failing to melt a heap of snow. Du Bo shook his head, murmuring that friendship was the second most important thing after family. He heard Fred mutter that no, for some, family came last. Du Bo tried to make sense of it, but was too tired to dwell on it.

Du Bo had decided that he would get up early in the morning to call around and see if any of his contacts knew of a Ning Fu. If someone could afford to buy a stolen artefact, he must surely be rich and well-known in the city.

'Du Bo,' JJ said, 'before we go to the hotel, I need to pick something up at the fine arts academy.'

'Do you have an address?' Fred asked before Du Bo could reply.

JJ only remained silent.

Du Bo closed his eyes again, but lay awake worrying about the two friends, well, former friends. Their falling out might derail the plan. He had noticed that Fred's actions were quicker than his thoughts, nothing unusual for a young, impulsive man. But Du Bo's mind kept offering images of Fred running away with the helmet, just to spite JJ. And if Du Bo could not witness the sale of the helmet and denounce the buyer as an enemy of the State, he would have to face dire consequences: lose his job, maybe even be sent to clean toilets in a remote province.

***

It was nine o'clock in the morning when Du Bo finally reached an old friend, Chang Wangyi.

'Ah, Du Bo, you are in Shanghai? Come visit me in the office. We go out for lunch,' said Du Bo's friend, glad to have company and an excuse to drink. 'Do you know where the Shanghai Municipal Party Committee Propaganda Bureau is?'

'I know, I know. But maybe another day. What about tomorrow? Today I am busy, but I wanted to know if you were in Shanghai. I did not want to miss the opportunity to see you.'

'Tomorrow? Yes, of course. Better dinner then. Lunchtime, I already have an appointment with the secretary of the sport committee.'

'Fine, fine. Lao Chang, I wonder if you could do me a favour.'

'Tell me.'

'I am doing research here on behalf of my work unit, and someone has told me that the person who is informed about the issue at hand is a certain Ning Fu,' said Du Bo, surprised that the lie came out quite naturally. 'I know a Ning, a Ning Hui, but I don't know if they are relatives.' Du Bo's prepared speech was so planned that his friend would think he was looking for someone to introduce him to Ning Fu himself.

'Oh, Ning Fu moves in the upper circles. I am just an insignificant party member here. I do not know anybody who knows him. I'm afraid I cannot help you.'

*Bingo*! Du Bo thought. *Ning Fu must be a high-calibre personality if just mentioning his name sufficed to identify him.*

'I see, I see. In which unit does he work? Is he from Shanghai?'

'I think his family is originally from Hangzhou. They were in the silk trade. The parents still live in Hangzhou. They sold all the shops, of course, but they still have a sort of mansion, and it is rumoured that the father still indirectly controls one of the best silk factories there. Does your research have something to do with that? Did those in Beijing finally get wind of his activities here? More than one would be happy to see him fall, but so far nobody has succeeded.'

Du Bo thanked his friend for the information and, without telling him much more, he arranged to meet him the next day at six pm in front of his office. Du Bo hoped his friend could be an ally when he would denounce Ning Fu.

***

In the hotel room, JJ had also woken up early, and had found a piece of paper and a pen.

*Dear George,*
    *Since the last time I wrote, my life has become a*

*complete mess. Fred doesn't talk to me because I want to go to the police to report the loss of my passport, Du Bo only cares about the buyer and getting credit for denouncing him, Roger only cares about money, the luggage is gone, the urn is gone, and I have no way to keep my promise to Old Min, or even contact his daughter. Why do I always take the wrong decisions? I thought going with Fred meant that this time nobody would get hurt because of my selfishness, but the truth is, I followed him and missed the ship in Hong Kong for the same reason I followed those kids in Phnom Penh. I just wanted to be accepted and…*

JJ squeezed his eyes tight to keep his tears from following. He realised only now, putting his thoughts on paper, what all that meant. He felt like he was melting from the inside, seeing himself again as a young, lonely child, as if time had never passed.

The old wooden door opened with a crack and Du Bo came in.

'What are you doing, JJ?' Du Bo asked, seeing him with his pen and paper, but eyes shut.

'I am writing to my cousin,' JJ said, opening his eyes.

'He is writing to his dead cousin,' said Fred with a grimace, only now getting up.

JJ stopped writing. 'Why do you have to say that?'

Fred shrugged.

'What do you care?' JJ insisted.

'C'est bien, it's nice. JJ thinks about his cousin,' Du Bo felt obliged to say.

'Yeah, sure… the guy is more friendly to dead people than to the living. Just saying… ' Fred told Du Bo.

Du Bo saw JJ's eyes getting wet. 'Bié chăole le, no more fighting. We still have work to do,' Du Bo said, hoping to put a stop to their bickering.

JJ passed his hands over his face, as if he had just awakened. In the last few days, he felt as if he had not been his usual self and that his body had been snatched by a stranger who lied, stole, and put his life at risk. He got up and went to the window. The air was already warm, with the temperature reaching twenty degrees. He could see the tenants of the houses in front. A woman was hanging her wet laundry on a wooden pole, which she then extended out of her window and into the humidity. Birds were singing, but there were none flying around. The sound came instead from small wooden cages down in the street, where two men were chatting, holding their cages with one hand. After a short while, one man resumed his morning walk, taking his bird cage with him. Life downstairs seemed quiet and relaxed.

The face of his cousin surged forth from the back of his mind, followed by the image of Old Min in hospital, his face aged and his breathing laboured. JJ's hands started trembling, and his eyes ached with unwanted tears. *I am a failure. I left George dying, I lost Old Min's ashes, I am letting Fred down.* JJ rushed outside to hide his distress. The living room downstairs was silent and empty; he threw himself on one of the lacquered chairs, his knee banging on the wooden armrest, bringing out a small cry of pain.

That was how Madame Sun found JJ: his hands holding his knee, his forehead on his hands, and tears running slowly down his face. She sat down quietly and waited for him to notice her silent presence.

After a few minutes, he startled when he noticed he was not alone. He quickly dried his eyes with his sleeve.

She was again heavily made up, her small eyes were

still cold as she spoke in a neutral voice. 'You are in trouble.'

'Yes,' he said. Her piercing eyes took away all his courage. 'It… it is too much for me… ' he said, shaking his head.

'Why upset?' Madame Sun asked.

'I think… I think of my cousin George. He died when he was just a child.'

'How die?'

'I… I was playing with some kids at their house, the kids of our maid, and my mother and my aunt were looking for me. They left my cousin, who was bitten by a poisonous snake. When they finally found me, my cousin had been bleeding from all orifices… '

'No doctor?'

'We were in Indochina, during the war. Not many doctors there. When they found one, it was too late.'

'Ah, Indochina. The war… Bad things happen. Long time ago. Why be sad now? Not useful.' She lost interest in the conversation and got up.

JJ looked at her, his eyes still red from crying, and said, 'I shouldn't have played with those kids, should I? If my mother and aunt were not looking for me, my cousin would still be alive.'

'Maybe yes, maybe no. Nobody know. But past is past, only fools cry for the past.' Madame Sun walked towards the door.

'Please, don't go! Stay for a while.'

She turned around to see this young lǎowài, one foot on the floor, one on the chair, his arms hugging his leg, serving as a protective shield. 'You tell me more interesting thing, I stay. You talk the past, I go.'

'Okay, okay.'

She went back and sat next to him. 'Why you in Shanghai?'

'I promised my old teacher to bring his ashes to his daughter and... ' He caught himself before telling her about the scroll.

'Mmm?'

... and we missed the boat, and I arrived too late. We should have arrived in Shanghai a week ago. Now I don't have the ashes.' Her lack of a reaction made him doubt he had spoken at all. He remained silent for a moment, rocking his body left and right. 'Do you think it is okay to leave a friend in need?' JJ asked.

'Which need? If friend in need, I maybe can help. You have money?' Madame Sun asked.

He shook his head vigorously, to stave off any ideas she might have formed in her head. 'No, no. I'm only saying this because my friend is... is lovesick and he needs a friend.'

Her eyes moved around JJ's face, looking right through him. 'Lovesick, I help. Many beautiful ladies here. But no money, no help.' She shrugged and finally got up to leave him alone.

JJ thought about her words. Only fools cry for the past, she said, but he was crying for the present too. He raised his head from his knee. The future was uncertain, but he could still change it. He only had to do the right thing.

# Chapter 27

At the train station, Du Bo went to buy his ticket; yesterday, he had already gone to two different ticket windows to buy two other tickets for JJ and Fred with his identity card. What he did was, of course, not allowed, but fortunately, the crowd at the station was so large, the employees at the counter could not possibly remember the faces of all ticket-buyers.

The journey was just a few hours, so he got the three of them hard seats. Their carriage was made up of a pair of benches facing each other, with a table in the middle. A small spittoon sat on each table. Often, four or more passengers occupied the bench, whose size could have accommodated only three people. Pieces of luggage were everywhere, as were piles of discarded seed coatings of different colours.

Again, JJ and Fred felt the persistent stares of the fellow passengers, but this time, they could not escape into their own cabin. Several passengers approached Du Bo and asked him about the two lǎowài. Du Bo always answered noncommittally that he did not know them and that he had just helped them find their way in the station. He thus avoided speaking to the two for the whole trip and concentrated on reading his newspaper.

Fred and JJ were silent as well, as they stubbornly refused to talk to each other. The seats were highly uncomfortable, and the air in the carriage sticky and unbreathable, despite the open windows. They looked with envy at the few women who were cooling themselves with colourful folding fans.

Shortly before arriving in Hangzhou, Du Bo got up to get his luggage, shooting a quick look at JJ to follow. Getting off the train was no less complicated than getting on, with people pushing in all directions towards the exit; when they finally were out, JJ sighed loudly. Du Bo seemed to be unruffled by the crowd, the noise, and the discomfort.

'How can you be so peaceful in this crowd? There are people everywhere, queues are so long, and you needed two extra hours to buy a ticket!' JJ said, glad to utter a few words again.

Du Bo looked a little surprised; he said it was France that was rather uncommon. Even the poorest people seemed to enjoy enough space to move and breathe, even on trains.

'We Chinese are many. People cannot all stay home,' he replied, 'so some go to work, some take trains, some wait for the bus… ' He laughed, but neither JJ nor Fred joined him.


Du Bo bought a map of the city and checked the location of the academy and of the hotel. Luckily, they were not far apart, and they could walk there. They agreed they would not enter the lobby together; Du Bo would go in first and act as if he was waiting for someone. JJ and Fred would come in a few minutes later, so Du Bo could see Ning Fu coming into the hotel. After that, Du Bo would leave the hotel and wait for them outside.

Both the academy and the hotel were near West Lake, and they followed Du Bo as he hastened towards the famous attraction.

'The lake, you must see the lake. Maybe after, we can go take a walk around the lake,' Du Bo said, his mood visibly lifted.

'We might not have the time to do so. We must go to the train station to meet Roger's Chinese friend to give him the money,' JJ said, holding the scroll to his chest with both hands. His mother had kept her word, somehow, and the handover of the precious painting at the academy went as smooth as his first days at sea. He hugged the long tube, grateful that at least one thing had worked out and hopeful that it was not the last. He had at least partly accomplished the mission from Old Min. Thanks to his mother's help.

***

Du Bo went inside the Hangzhou Friendship Hotel and scanned the lobby as if he were looking for someone, then he went to sit on one of the couches, not too far from the reception desk. His heart was beating fast. It was not unusual for him to go meet someone in a hotel lobby, only this time it was a much nicer hotel. The cream-coloured leather of the couch felt smooth under his touch, and small tables with lamps illuminated a pair of large vases. The elegant atmosphere was enhanced by the quiet; only two other men were in the lobby, talking and smoking in one corner. Du Bo scratched his neck nervously and cleared his throat repeatedly.

A few minutes later, JJ and Fred entered, with the precious helmet in a bag in JJ's hands. They also looked around, and as nobody approached them, they sat on one of the couches. The men in the corner had the time to smoke two more cigarettes before a well-dressed woman walked towards JJ and Fred; she only spoke Chinese, but held up a small piece of paper with the word 'Roger' on it.

Du Bo could see that JJ and Frew were as taken aback

as he was to find that their contact was a woman, but the two Frenchmen agreed to follow her. Du Bo swore under his breath. He kept waiting in the lobby, hoping Ning Fu would come later. But in the end, he only saw JJ and Fred return, their bag replaced with a much larger one.

Du Bo hurried to meet them outside.

'What happened?' he asked.

'Nothing. It all went as planned. We showed him the goods, he called Roger on the phone while we counted the money. When we finished, we swapped our bags and that's it,' JJ answered.

'What was he like? Was he already there?' Du Bo asked.

'No, he came after. We waited fifteen minutes alone in the room. You did not see him?'

'No! He did not go through the lobby,' replied Du Bo, grasping the hair on his head. 'Tell me how he looked like,' he urged, without thinking how pointless it was. The description would not help him in the least. He had expected this Ning Fu to arrive through the lobby, and Du Bo had planned to ask the reception to confirm his identity, or even find an excuse to go talk to him on his way out. And now? Would he still be able to pull off his plan?

The three men walked silently to the train station.

'Are you still going ahead with your plan, Du Bo?' JJ asked, concerned.

Du Bo shook his shoulders slightly and said, 'Yes, I have to. It would have been better to see him and have proof, but... ' He did not finish his sentence, recreating in his head the scene he was supposed to play out with Ning Fu at the hotel. He was ready with an excuse to go talk to him, and looking at the bulging bag with Ning Fu, Du Bo would innocently ask what he had there. Of course, he was not expecting Ning Fu to show the helmet to him, but he had hoped to see a certain embarrassment in his face and manners, which Du Bo could then report to the police as suspicious.

Du Bo turned to JJ and reassured him again that he would be fine. At the entrance of the station, they stopped.

'Well, I wish you good luck,' JJ said. 'Thank you for your help.' He turned to Fred, expecting him to say something, too.

'Yes, thank you,' Fred said, like a child who had been forced to say 'hello' to a distant old aunt.

'You two should look after each other, be good friends,' Du Bo said, seeing that the mood between JJ and Fred was still gloomy.

'Yeah, sure, we heard you. Friends are important,' Fred said, his hands in his trouser pockets as he looked around, unconcerned by the conversation.

JJ's lips were stretched in a tight smile, which betrayed his hurt at Fred's implicit reproach. Du Bo shifted his weight from one foot to the other, embarrassed to say more.

'Be careful, and may you reach Hong Kong safely,' Du Bo said, shaking JJ's hand. He offered his hand to Fred too, who took it nonchalantly, but this time making eye contact with Du Bo.

After saying their goodbyes, JJ and Fred found Cai Jun waiting near the entrance. Du Bo left the two friends with Cai Jun and entered the train station, so disappointed that he completely forgot about his earlier wish to see the West Lake.

'You, come,' Cai Jun said to the two Frenchmen, and he led them to his car, which was parked in a quiet place behind the station. They all got in and lowered their heads while the driver stood outside, moving side to side to cover the movements inside.

JJ passed the money to Cai Jun, who counted it carefully. He sighed loudly, took some bills, and gave them to JJ and Fred. 'Now, out.'

'You are going to Guangzhou, aren't you? Can't we go back with you?' JJ asked.

'No, no, not okay,' Cai Jun said and motioned his driver to help. The car door opened, and the driver grabbed Fred's arm to pull him out, then JJ.

'Hey, no need to be so rude. We got it,' Fred said.

The two were left staring at the car as it disappeared from sight.

'Now what?' JJ said.

This time Fred replied. 'You are the smart one who always knows best. You find a way we can travel to Guangzhou.'

JJ looked at the money, as he had no wish to see Fred's mocking face. 'Right. Let's go back to the Friendship Hotel.'

# Chapter 28

Back in Shanghai, Du Bo was on his way to a simple restaurant to meet with Chang Wangyi. He had spent the train journey from Hangzhou rehearsing his story and came up with a friendly approach to find out more about Ning Fu. The restaurant looked like a canteen and was full and very loud inside.

'How are things going, Du Bo? You look beaten.'

'Do you remember I asked you about Ning Fu?' Du Bo replied, not wasting any time.

'Yes, of course. Is Beijing after him?' Wangyi asked, his voice betraying a certain expectation.

'No, not yet, at least. But it came to my knowledge that he may have done something illegal. Something awfully bad. And my plan is to denounce him.'

Wangyi banged his fist on the table, adding to the general noise of the place. 'It would not be the first time he has done something illegal; that bastard always has somebody to cover it up. What is it this time?'

'He purchased an artefact that had been pillaged from a tomb belonging to the museum in Changsha.'

Wangyi's mouth opened in disbelief, then he shook his head in disapproval. Grabbing his pack of cigarettes, he offered one to Du Bo, who took it. Both lost in their own thoughts, the two men smoked and looked at each other. Wangyi waited for Du Bo to say more, but when he didn't, he asked him what the stolen good was.

'A beautiful ancient jade helmet, hundreds of small white plates with tiny holes kept together by a thin, almost invisible thread.'

'Sounds beautiful. How do you know? Did you see it?'

Du Bo bit his tongue at his stupidity and rushed to reply that he just saw a picture of it somewhere in the paper.

They discussed the value of the piece, quite a large sum for both of the men, then drifted from the topic, and spent a good portion of their meal dreaming about what they could do with the money—knowing, of course, being rich in communist China was not a good idea.

'So how and to whom are you going to denounce him?' Wangyi asked, putting another morsel of sliced cold chicken into his mouth.

'I don't know. I also have no proof.'

His friend put his chopsticks down in surprise and in disbelief. 'What are you saying? We've been discussing this crime here the whole time and you have no proof? How do you think they are going to believe you?'

Du Bo also stopped eating and tried to explain how he got the information, without mentioning his involvement with JJ and Fred. He had prepared a story, and telling it now would test its credibility.

'It happened like so: while I was travelling to Beijing, I was in the same carriage as two lǎowài, from France. I had spent some time in France so I could understand the language a little. I overheard them discuss a sale with a certain Ning Fu and were directed first to Shanghai, then to Hangzhou to bring the buyer the helmet. Of course, they did not know that I could speak the language. I remembered I had read an article about stolen artefacts from a tomb, so I followed them around. I know they sold the piece; they went to the hotel with a bag containing the object and they left with another one, probably containing the money. I know who they sold it to, but Ning Fu did not go through the lobby, thus I did

217

not see him.'

'What? Two foreigners are involved in this? Who are they? Where did they go?'

'I don't know who they are. I barely spoke a few words with them, and they were not very friendly. I also did not want them to notice that I was following them. But I can assure you that they sold the helmet and that the buyer was Ning Fu.'

'But how can you be so sure if you did not see him?' asked his friend, who had resumed eating.

'The lǎowài did not know that I could understand them. They spoke quite freely between themselves.'

'But you said you spoke to them?'

Du Bo bit his tongue and corrected himself. 'Yes, but just a few words in Chinese: hello, how are you. One of them spoke some Chinese.' Du Bo was sweating under his shirt, but he continued his story. 'I had no reason to speak with them and they paid me no attention.' He paused a moment to swallow some rice, along with his saliva. 'When I heard what they were discussing, I refrained from speaking with them, so they would keep talking openly in front of me and I could hear their plan.'

Wangyi nodded and seemed to believe the story. Du Bo's slippery hands let the chopsticks fall on the floor, and he urged the waiter to bring a clean pair.

'You did not get their names?'

'How could I? You don't usually mention the name of a friend you are talking to, do you? How often did you mention my name tonight?' Du Bo retorted.

'You are right, you are right.' He was pensive and was eating at a slow pace now. 'This is a weird story. How did these lǎowài get the helmet? Were they spy?'

'I don't know. They already had the object with them.'

'From where did you take the train?'

'Guangzhou.'

'So they stole the object in Changsha and brought it to Guangzhou and then travelled to Shanghai?' asked Wangyi, a little sceptical.

'What do I know? Maybe they got it later. That I did not see. I knew which train they were supposed to take in Changsha, and I took the same. What they did that afternoon before leaving Changsha, I cannot say.' One of Du Bo's chopsticks fell again from the table, but he caught it midair.

'Ning Fu is a powerful man. You have no proof. It is your word against his. I don't know what you expect.'

'He bought an illegal artefact that belongs to the people. 'Uncover whatever secret and harmful action by reactionary elements.' This is what Chairman Mao says. This is not only illegal, but the question is also how he got so much money to buy it.'

'Yes, but Chairman Mao also says, 'Those who protect bandits and spies must be punished.'

'That is my point exactly,' Du Bo said, failing to see the connection his friend just made. 'If he bought the object, he must have it somewhere. Of course, I cannot prove it myself, but if I report it, the authority can search his house. They cannot protect him.'

Wangyi emitted a long sigh. 'How naïve you are. You don't really think they will go that far?'

'Why should they not? Why should his word count more than mine? Why would I lie?'

'Exactly because he has the kind of money to buy such a thing and you don't. This is why his word counts more.'

'Maybe that was true before, but we are now living in another era. This is the new China and the government surely does not tolerate such things now!'

'You wish… '

They both fell silent. Du Bo resented what his friend

was implying. He drank his glass of beer and poured himself another one, purposely skipping over Wangyi's empty glass, as would be custom, indirectly affirming that times had changed and that old customs were not relevant anymore.

'What now? Do you really think you can fight such a person? Go ahead, be my guest. But don't tell me later that I did not warn you.'

The two old friends parted shortly after dinner. It was too late to go to the authorities. Nobody important would be there to listen to his story, so Du Bo went to find a hotel to stay for the night. He dragged his tired feet on the pavement, carrying his luggage with him. His friend had instilled doubt in him, but what other options had he now? He still believed that times had changed and that Chairman Mao supported the people and was against those harming the country. And wasn't having so much money to buy such a valuable artefact, a stolen artefact, the same as harming the motherland? *I am just denouncing a counterrevolutionary,* Du Bo thought. *There is no material gain for me. They have to believe me.* The police or whoever was responsible for investigating such theft only needed to look for the helmet. It wasn't a small object; surely, it would be found.

\*\*\*

Fred walked in silence a step behind JJ as they headed back to the Friendship Hotel. Glaring at JJ's back, Fred felt that he was supposed to be the main character in this journey to Asia, but was increasingly playing the sidekick. He had been the one who went on the adventure, yet JJ was taking over all the decisions. JJ had not trusted him, had told him what to do and what not to do; JJ even gave away Fred's watch, the one he borrowed from his father without his knowledge. He did not like being the sidekick. *Right, JJ's kicks under the table back in Guangzhou*. Fred had not liked that either. He should have kicked JJ back instead of shutting his mouth, yes… then JJ would not have been so bossy.

At the hotel, Fred walked away from the reception desk and found a seat, getting as far as possible from JJ and his attempt to get train tickets from the hotel staff. Fred heard him say 'urgent', 'stolen passport', 'departing ship', and scoffed. Fred would not have bothered with explanations; he would have simply showed the bonehead at the desk the money and demanded a ticket, no discussions.

JJ's method worked, eventually. *After much more explanation than was necessary*, Fred thought.

Still, they had their tickets and hours later had boarded the train and found their cabin, which this time was theirs for most of the journey. The heavy atmosphere only got heavier when the doors closed and the train took off for the long trip to Guangzhou.

Fred spent his time sleeping or looking out the window. It was a pity JJ was such a righteous person. Fred had had fun on the ship with him, but if JJ did not want to talk to him, Fred would not talk either.

Their friendship had been like a brief love affair— not that he had much experience in the field—as the intense bonding in their early days changed into resentment and distrust at the first signs of trouble. It would have been so easy to release the tension, maybe just one word would have done it, but Fred was not going to speak first. JJ had to, if he cared.

A few hours later Fred's stomach started complaining about the lack of food. He stretched a hand towards JJ. 'Give me some money. I am hungry.'

Without comment, JJ handed over some bills and Fred disappeared. He returned half an hour later with one lunchbox and a bottle of rice wine, which he put noisily on the table. Fred expected JJ to say something as he ate, but he just looked incredulous. After he was full, Fred climbed into the upper berth and lay down, letting the rift between them get wider.

# Chapter 29

The office of the provincial first party secretary was in an old mansion with high ceilings and large windows, close to the old French concession. Du Bo had not planned to take the matter this high, but after the police did not take him seriously, he did not know where he could go.

He was now in a waiting room on one of its cheap chairs, twisting his blue cap in his hands. Civil servants were coming and going through a door to what Du Bo thought was the party secretary's office; each time someone came out, he expected to be called in but was not.

After almost an hour, a thin employee accompanied him to the desk of a man slightly younger than himself. Du Bo read his name and his position on the nameplate on the table, and he felt relieved that he had not been brought to the provincial first party secretary himself.

'Tóngzhì, comrade, you have something important to say?' the man said with a friendly smile.

Du Bo felt his muscles relax and started telling his story. The man appeared to listen intently, leaning forward at times, and nodding and humming at other times, and even offered Du Bo a cup of hot water when Du Bo had a fit of coughing.

'You now know the matter at hand,' Du Bo finished. 'I went to the police, but they did not take me seriously. I know I have no formal proof, but should not my word be sufficient for an investigation? Chairman Mao says that 'he who harms the people will not easily escape justice.' '

'Of course, of course. We are all comrades working for the same goal. Why would you lie?' the man replied. He let Du Bo repeat the complete story again, while he took notes. In the end, the man promised that he would report the matter and that it would be taken care of. He asked Du Bo not to leave the city because they might have more questions for him.

That alarmed Du Bo. 'Bù tài fāngbiàn, it is not very convenient. I delayed my departure to report this matter. I must go back to Beijing. My unit is waiting for me.'

'Sure, we understand. We won't bring you much more inconvenience but we need your cooperation now. Write the address where you are staying here; we will get in touch with you soon. Don't worry.'

\*\*\*

Yvette paced back and forth in her living room, looking nervously at the clock on the wall. JJ's train would have arrived by now. When he had called from the train station the previous day, she had told him to hire a rickshaw to bring him to Shamian. The small island was well known and even if the rickshaw driver did not know the location of the church, it would be easy to find just by walking around. She had found that the Chinese sometimes had a peculiar habit of not understanding a foreigner speaking Mandarin, their brain somehow not being able to reconcile the unusual combination.

She glanced at the clock again and her worry increased. She had read in the newspaper of people being stabbed to death and left bleeding on a side street, or even worse, being thrown into the Pearl River. In her confused state, she overlooked the fact that there were likely no quiet side streets to leave a stabbed man at this hour of the day. One could not take more than a few steps alone along the river without encountering somebody fishing or walking.

When the doorbell finally rang, Yvette grinned and rushed to open it. When her eyes focused on Xiao Lin, who had returned from the market, Yvette's expression changed back to distress. Xiao Lin only looked at her with curiosity.

The weather was already quite hot for that time of the year, and despite it still being early morning, the air in the flat was sticky. Yvette did not enjoy cooking when it was so hot and humid, but she joined Xiao Lin in the kitchen, nevertheless. That morning, her restlessness made the kitchen chores particularly challenging, and she accidentally cut her index finger with the large knife. She placed her finger in her mouth to prevent the blood from spilling on the floor and went to the bedroom to find the small bottle of alcohol for cleaning the wound. Dabbing her finger with the liquid, a wave of burning pain washed over her and she frowned. She glimpsed her reflection in the mirror. She turned her back on it and sat on the bed, keeping her finger pressed with her other hand. Her breathing was shallow and fast, matching the speed of the thoughts popping up in her head.

The truth was that she had not stopped thinking about JJ since she first met him. She felt torn between guilt for even imagining a different life, one in which her husband Kurt had no place, and the excitement she felt. In the past few days, she caught herself laughing out loud while picturing meeting JJ again. This new feeling made her more lively, so much so that even her husband had once asked if something was wrong with her. She lied to him, to this man who had always treated her so well.

The doorbell rang again, making her jump. She wiped her eyes quickly with the back of her hand and strained her ears to hear who was at the door greeting Xiao Lin.

\*\*\*

The first bang on the door sufficed to wake Du Bo. He had slept deeply and peacefully after his visit to the provincial first party secretary's office yesterday. He had gone to bed feeling relieved and very pleased with himself. He had contributed to making China a better place, and now he did not have to worry about losing his position. Maybe he would even get a promotion.

The second knock on the door was louder and more urgent, and more banging came before Du Bo could get up to open the door. Two policemen stood in the doorway.

'Are you Du Bo, working in the agricultural machinery unit in Beijing?' one of them asked.

'Yes, I am. What is it?'

'Get dressed, pack your things, and come with us,' the same policeman said.

'Yes, of course.' He had expected the police to come and ask him questions, but not so early in the morning. While packing his luggage, he wondered why he had to take his belongings with him. He hoped they were not here just to put him on a train back to Beijing without investigating the case.

Only later, when he would spend the day in a jail cell, would he wish they had.

***

After a flickering hesitation, Yvette greeted JJ and Fred warmly at the door, dispelling any initial awkwardness. With cups of diluted coffee in front of them, JJ and Fred recounted their trip to Yvette, who listened with a quiet smile. Their retelling was like pieces of a puzzle, each of their experiences told from a different angle. But instead of having a complete picture, many pieces did not seem to fit together. At a certain point, Yvette asked why they were not looking at each other. Both friends fell silent.

'You have quarrelled?' she asked.

Neither JJ nor Fred replied.

'That's silly. You were such good friends,' she said, shaking her head.

At lunchtime, the three of them discussed with Father Kurt how to best leave China.

Father Kurt dashed JJ's hopes of finding a legal way out. 'These are difficult times for foreigners in China. Reporting the loss of your documents will cause the authorities to check when you entered the country. If they find none, they will suspect you to be a spy. Should they somehow get wind you were involved with the stolen artefact, you are likely to face a prison sentence or worse,' Father Kurt added.

'Can we get somebody to make us counterfeit passports?' Fred asked.

JJ turned his eyes upwards in irritation but did not comment.

'Why not?' Fred insisted. 'I have seen foreigners in Shanghai. You are also foreign. We could easily take the identity of two foreigners living in China. And since they don't like foreigners, they should be happy to let us go.'

Father Kurt shook his head.

'First of all, I am sure you understand that in my role, I do not have those kinds of contacts. Second, they may not like foreigners, but they are keen to get their hands on whatever property and wealth they have. They put in place an exit system for foreigners, and this would not be less dangerous for you. Stories are circulating about how foreigners have a very narrow window to leave, sometimes from a different port than the one closest to home. The notice rarely allows them to settle all their business before leaving; often personal wealth and belongings are confiscated with the excuse that they must contribute to help build the new China.

'Your only option is to go through smugglers again. Do you still have contacts with your Chinese friend or the one from Hong Kong?'

JJ was afraid he would say that. 'The Chinese man was not our friend; he is Roger's partner. I am not sure that Roger can help us without the cooperation of his partner. And the guy does not want to help us.'

'I see.' Father Kurt paused a moment to think. 'I know fishermen on the coast often smuggle goods and people to Tai O; it is not without risk, and even if I know of this, I do not have any contacts myself.'

'Tai O? Where is that?' JJ asked.

'It's on Lantau Island, one of the bigger islands belonging to the colony. I gather it takes about two days to reach Hong Kong Island from there, but it will be much easier for you once you are in the British colony. There should be a police post and you can ask for help.' Father Kurt told the men he would talk to his church assistant, Lao Wu. He heard that in the past some Christians have left the country with help, and Lao Wu might know more.

\*\*\*

After spending nearly the whole day in a jail cell with no explanation, an agent finally brought Du Bo into a bare room to face a comrade, an interrogator.

'Tóngzhì, tell us your story,' the man said, stressing the word for 'comrade'.

'I was on the train with two Frenchmen, travelling towards Beijing. I can understand French and overheard their conversation.'

'Why can you understand French?'

'I stayed in France for a while.'

'Why did you stay in a foreign country? When? What were you doing there?'

Du Bo felt the questions were not truly relevant, but he patiently answered them.

'Why did you not want to work in China? You don't love your motherland?'

'Yes, of course I do. That's why I came back to fight for China's independence.'

'But you tried to leave first. Which contacts did you have there? Who sent you back here?'

The questions about his past dug deeper into his involvement in the war and in the party. Du Bo felt extremely uncomfortable; only on the second day of his interrogation was he allowed to tell his story.

At first, he tried to explain the case and the circumstances under which he came to know about the theft, passing over his travels and brief friendship with JJ and Fred. But the lack of proper sleep and food had taken a toll on him, and he ended up telling the interrogator the entire story of his encounter with the foreigners. He confessed he was present when the helmet was bought and indirectly assisted the foreigners to sell it, by arranging the trip to Hangzhou. He hoped that by telling the full story, he would restore his credibility, which his interrogators seemed to doubt. Once he told them everything, they could not but believe him, he thought. They would then go after Ning Fu.

Instead, the police regarded his passive involvement in the sale and purchase of the helmet and his cooperation with two foreigners as highly illicit: Du Bo was charged and found guilty of conspiracy with foreign agents, with the aim of committing crimes against the government, and of complicity in art theft.

# Chapter 30

The next day, Father Kurt found his assistant busy sorting the church candles and melting together the short ones to form new candles. Father Kurt thought it was a good time to bring up the matter of the smugglers.

'Tell me, Lao Wu, how was the situation for the Christians during the war?' he asked in English.

'Same like others, they no have special treatment,' Lao Wu said.

'But did they have worse treatment? Were they persecuted?'

'If persecuted, I no hear it.' Lao Wu placed the wax in a tall copper pot and ignited a small gas cooker.

'I heard a few families had trouble, lost their jobs and such,' insisted Father Kurt.

'During war, all lost job. No difference.' Lao Wu was not very cooperative. Father Kurt had often complained to Yvette about how tiring it was to have longer conversations with Lao Wu, and the couple used to discuss whether Lao Wu did it on purpose to keep them at a distance or whether his English was worse than it sounded.

'I see, I see. I suppose many fled to Hong Kong to find jobs?' Father Kurt said, trying a more direct way.

'Eh, Hong Kong, no easy. Many people look fortune, they no find.' Lao Wu looked at the wax that was slowly melting. 'Like candles.'

Father Kurt looked at him, puzzled.

'Yes, like candles. Go to Hong Kong, new life like wax melt, have nothing, no shape. Some wax become new candle, some wax stick to pot and go to bin.'

Father Kurt had to laugh at his assistant's far-reaching metaphor. 'Sure, sure. Not everybody will succeed. It is the will of God.'

'God will or will triads. If you money, much better. No money, you probably stick to pot,' Lao Wu solemnly said.

'Yes, the triads. Are there many operating on the coast of Guangzhou?'

'Who know? Many. But before, many, many, many. Then they went to Taiwan and only many were left.'

To Lao Wu, 'many' was an indefinite amount, which only sometimes matched the meaning foreigners had for the word. More than once, Lao Wu told Father Kurt that many parishioners were present at Mass, only for Father Kurt to discover a sparse group of six or seven people.

'Did my predecessor help Christians leave the country?' Father Kurt asked.

'Oh yes, of course. It was Wang family, three generations. Ah, what disaster… ' Lao Wu said.

'Disaster? Why?' Father Kurt asked, following Lao Wu around the church while he was busy with his tasks.

'They caught from Hong Kong police, after paying large money to passers. Police fired, sampan go in water, almost all die.'

'So dangerous, was it?'

'No, no, but family Wang stupid family. They insisted go with many furniture, sampan too slow for police. Results not good: no furniture, no money, no grandma, and those who alive got a cold, very bad, could have die from cold.'

Father Kurt pointed out that a serious cold was still better than drowning.

'Bad cold also you could die,' Lao Wu said, nodding.

'How did they find someone to help them cross?'

Father Kurt asked.

'Gone to village where fishermen fish in the sea and ask around.'

'Father Guglielmo just went and asked around? Just like that?'

'People know who cross. Common fact. You ask, they tell you who cross. Just like here. All know where church is, also if no come to church,' Lao Wu said, laughing.

Father Kurt took a deep breath and, lowering his voice, he said, 'I have to tell you something. I have two guests with me who need help to go to Hong Kong.' He hoped that Lao Wu would understand without his having to spell it out.

'Méi wèntí! No problem! Brother-in-law my older brother cousin is good friend, I talk to him,' Lao Wu said, now taking a broom to sweep the church floor.

'Brother-in-law of your cousin?' Father Kurt said, translating the relationship in Western terms.

'No, no, dàgē no real brother. His cousin no my cousin. But his cousin brother-in-law my good pal,' Lao Wu replied matter-of-factly. 'When need go to Hong Kong?'

'As soon as possible,' replied Father Kurt, glad to see the matter could be so easily arranged.

\*\*\*

Yvette was sitting in an armchair mending some clothing as JJ studied a map of China that Father Kurt had given him. It was just the two of them. Fred had taken the chance, again, to go to the market with Xiao Lin.

JJ found the British colony on the map and looked for Lantau and Tai O. After the crossing, they expected to land on an island further away from the bustling Victoria Harbour; from there, they had to reach the more civilised and connected part of Hong Kong.

JJ looked at the clock on the wall for the hundredth time, but its hands seemed to move at a snail's pace. It was still too early to call his mother. He needed money. The yuan Cai Jun gave them in Hangzhou was not sufficient to pay for the passage, and, reluctantly, they had to borrow money from Father Kurt, which JJ did with little grace after Yvette talked him into it.

'Do you always spend your time mending? When we first arrived, you were mending as well,' JJ asked.

Yvette looked up, startled. 'Oh, no. But there are always pieces of clothing or linen that need some mending and I suppose it is a spouse's job to do such things.'

'You suppose?'

'As I said, my mother died in childbirth. Nobody taught me about being married. I just do what I see other women doing.'

'I don't think I ever saw my mother mending anything in her life.'

'She never did?'

'Never. Okay, my family is well off and my mother did not have to do the housework herself, but she also did not care about staying at home and just being a wife. I told you already how she looked for a job as a teacher as soon as we got to Phnom Penh. And back in France, she started working there too.'

'Maybe it is good, but why work if you then neglect your child?' she said, then she blushed apologetically. 'Did you call her?' Yvette asked, to cover her embarrassment.

'Yes, she helped me to contact Old Min's friend at the school. He gave me the scroll. She sounded… worried on the phone.'

'Is that strange?'

'I told you, she never cared about me. She is divorcing my father,' he said in a single breath, as if he were expelling a fishbone stuck in his throat.

Yvette felt compelled to reach over and place her hand on his to comfort him. 'I'm sorry,' she offered quietly. 'Was your mother so unhappy with your father?'

Motionless, JJ stared into the void, unaware of her affectionate gesture. He had never thought about that. His parents were to him a single unit, like a pair of gloves or socks. He realised that happiness was not an interesting question to him; what love was concerned him more. Love between men and women, love between children and parents, between friends, and the more abstract love, the one he felt for the arts, or the one Du Bo felt for his country. Or love of money.

*Gosh*, he thought, *Fred, Roger, Du Bo, Cai Jun, Ning Fu, me… We are all in the same boat, all looking for something or someone to love…* He looked at Yvette, who stared at him with sad eyes, still waiting for a response. He concluded that his mother had married for love, but that her experiences had made her into another person, one who was not willing to live as a spectator of her own life. One whose life had no space for a child.

'You care about your mother. Have you ever told your mother that?' Yvette asked.

'No,' he said.

'Then maybe you are doing the same, who knows?' she said, sending JJ an inquiring look.

JJ shook his head, not able to believe that.

When Fred returned, he immediately ran to Yvette, almost falling into her arms, causing her to take a step back to avoid falling.

'Yvette, ask your maid to buy the newspaper,' Fred said, excited.

Yvette looked at him, failing to understand the reason. 'Which newspaper?'

'The one hanging on public display, in the side street next to the market. There is a picture of the helmet.' His voice was unusually shrill.

Yvette turned on the spot to grab a piece of paper as she shouted to Xiao Lin to come out of the kitchen. After jotting down a few characters in her childish handwriting, she handed the note to Xiao Lin. It simply said, 'Buy newspaper.' A halting conversation followed, as the maid did not know which one.

'She doesn't understand. I'll go get my husband's assistant, wait here,' Yvette said, and she ran out to the church.

'Fred, what do you think the article is about?' JJ asked him.

'I don't know, but I am afraid nothing good. While I was walking next to Xiao Lin, everybody turned around to look at me,' Fred said.

JJ's body seemed to relax a little. 'Nothing new there, you know how they do that.'

Fred put his hands on JJ's shoulders and, shaking his head, he said, 'No, it was worse. Different, I tell you. The girl stopped to greet someone. As I waited, I looked at the newspaper that was hanging nearby and saw something familiar. When I saw the picture, I could not hide my surprise. At that point, people stared at me and stepped back, as if I had the plague. This is different; usually they come and surround us with questions, but this time,' he again shook his head, worried, 'they were afraid.'

236

After Yvette communicated with Xiao Lin and the girl had come back with the newspaper, JJ, Fred, and Yvette flipped through the pages until they came to an article with a tiny black-and-white photo.

JJ jerked back when he saw it. 'That's the helmet! What does the article say?' JJ asked, frantic.

Yvette started reading slowly, reaching now and then for the dictionary to check the meaning of a word. After what to JJ and Fred seemed a long time, she summarised the brief article.

'A certain Du Bo has been arrested and charged for facilitating the theft of an art object. He is accused of selling it to two foreigners whose names are not known.'

'Du Bo. That's our friend from the train,' JJ said.

Yvette's eyes became darker and her voice dropped. 'He has been sentenced to the death penalty.'

JJ and Fred froze, unable to utter a word. They looked at each other, horrified. Their escape was now even more urgent. There was no way to know what Du Bo had revealed to the police under pressure, maybe even after being tortured.

*** 

Two days later, after Lao Wu had helped Father Kurt make all the arrangements, the time to cross was upon them. Without a chance to say their goodbyes to Yvette and Father Kurt, JJ and Fred were woken up in the middle of the night by Lao Wu and told to pack quickly. The two Frenchmen were only too eager to get on with it, and they grinned at each other, the first time they had done so in a long while. At that moment, they gave each other courage to face the unknown and banish the upsetting news about Du Bo.

Lao Wu took JJ and Fred to a fisherman's village

where the brother-in-law of his older cousin was waiting. Money exchanged hands, with Lao Wu taking a cut and leaving the two friends there with the contact. The village was still asleep, but closer to the seashore, the buzz of voices was a clear sign they were not the only ones awake that night.

As they approached the sea, JJ's and Fred's eyes adjusted to the darkness. The beach was a long and thin strip of pebbles and sand. They glimpsed a sampan nearby, but the moonless night made it hard to see anything clearly. Lao Wu's contact gently helped them into a smaller boat, which would bring them to the larger boat, and bade them goodbye.

JJ held a bamboo tube to his chest; the scroll was safely tucked inside it. Lao Wu's contact tried to convince JJ to leave it, in case it might hamper him if the trip became dangerous. JJ refused to let it go, however. The man did not say what kind of danger they were expecting, and both JJ and Fred naively assumed the worse they would have to do was run from the coast guards once the boat moored.

On their way to the coast, Lao Wu had described the crossing as a mere leisure trip, the fishermen were used to the waters. But when JJ and Fred stepped onto the sampan, they realised they had imagined a different kind of leisure boat trip. The sampan was full to bursting; there was no space to move among the people. The boat was being towed by another sampan, and eventually the wind picked up and increased the speed of the boat.

'I hope the wind is blowing in the right direction,' Fred said.

'Well, wherever we are going, we are going to get there faster,' JJ said, expressing a wish rather than a fact. He did not like how the boat was rocking. The sea was swelling and the people on the boat were nervous. He could not understand what was being said, but here and there he could hear sobbing.

A gigantic wave rocked the boat, splashing water inside, causing a loud cry among the passengers. JJ felt Fred grabbing his arm, his face was tense and pale.

'I cannot swim,' Fred said in panic. 'I cannot swim in the sea. I am afraid of the open sea.' His fingers were now white from the sheer pressure on JJ's arm.

'You will not need to swim, don't worry. The sea is a little rough, but it will be okay. We are not alone, should something happen,' JJ said, pointing with his chin at the sampan in front.

But at that point, their sampan laboriously lowered its sails and manoeuvred the other boat back towards the coast, leaving them alone to face the sea and its rolling waves.

In the following half-hour, the screams got louder with each successive wave; the mothers were yelling to their children not to let go, the children were weeping, and the men were trying to keep their families together, gripping with all their force ropes, poles, or anything that looked stable. Then came the agonising, desperate cries as first one, then two, then three children fell into the sea. These were the smaller children, those whose parents could not hold them because their hands were busy with other children, or the occasional elderly mother. Those whose tiny bodies could not stand up to the force of the waves and whose hands were too weak to hold on to life. Soon, the roaring of the sea overcame all shouts and cries, taking the older children, the adults, and the whole sampan into its deep, grey waters.

JJ and Fred plunged into the choppy waves, with JJ holding his friend by his shirt and struggling to keep Fred's head above the surface. The waves were still high, and they would occasionally go under, but JJ was glad he had learnt how to swim, only thanks to the boorish insistence of his father.

JJ scanned the debris that bobbed in the water here and there, and grabbed hold of a large one nearby. Another half an hour passed, but the sky was still dark. Around them the sea quietened; no more voices were heard, those who survived too exhausted to cry out loud. JJ tried to show Fred how to let the water support his body, but Fred was too stiff from the fear and the cold. His teeth were chattering, his lips were becoming blue, and his fingertips increasingly wrinkled.

The water was not excessively cold to JJ, who still felt strong enough to keep talking to help them stay awake and partially alert. He could not say how long they were there: he told Fred all about his life with an abundance of details, and all about his dreams, which he did not even know he had but which came to his mind right there and then, chasing away the thought that maybe he would not have the time to fulfil any of them. JJ told Fred about his mother, while he had little to say about his father. And then, he felt his eyes become heavy, and he started struggling with his words. He heard some cries and looked at the sky, and saw a few birds flying above them. He realised it was dawn, maybe his last one on earth.

# Chapter 31

The night the *Cambodge* left Hong Kong, Marcel realised that something was wrong only when Fred and JJ did not join him in their cabin when it was time to sleep. The next day, he immediately talked to the captain to ask for help and to look for them on the ship. After a fruitless search, the captain contacted the Hong Kong police to report their disappearance. In Shanghai, Marcel waited two days but when no further news came from Hong Kong, he went back, taking all the documents and luggages of both Fred and JJ with him.

He booked a room at the Four Seas hotel, a newish guesthouse that opened four years earlier, according to a leaflet somebody pressed into his hand at the harbour. It was on the Kowloon side, in front of Waterloo Hill, and its elegantly decorated entrance was above the street level. Marcel got a room with a balcony, from which he got a good view of the surroundings. Once settled in, he went to the Hong Kong police, hoping they would help him. To his disappointment, the police officer told him quite plainly that they had enough on their hands with the massive refugee influx from China and that one or two missing foreigners were not high on their priority list.

After a few of days of inaction, mostly spent in his hotel room smoking, he decided to ask for help from the French Commission.

'Your brother is an adult, and he left the ship on his own will. We understand your concern, but there is not much from our side that we can do,' a clerk at the commission told Marcel.

'He might have done it on his own will, but something must have happened to him. Isn't it someone's job to look for missing French citizens?'

'You should in this case go to the police.'

'I already went. They said they have no time.'

'Yes, they are quite busy. I know it is not a pleasant thought, but usually, when something like this happens, a body will eventually be found somewhere. If this has not been the case until now, there might be a chance your brother is alive and kicking.'

Grunting, Marcel left his contact at the hotel with the clerk in case the French Commission heard something.

A few days later, a call came to his hotel room.

'Mr Marechal, the French Commission speaking. Your brother has been found. He showed up in Tai O with his French friend. They almost drowned and your brother is in hospital, I was told by the Hong Kong police.'

'My gosh, at least he is alive. How is his state? What was he doing in Tai O? Where is this place?'

'Tai O is the haven for smugglers and triads. You'd have to talk to your brother to find out which one of these groups he belongs,' the voice on the phone said in a mocking tone.

Marcel replied he had nothing against either of them if they ensured his brother's survival.

'I have no further information on his state of health,' the voice said.

'How can I get to Tai O?' Marcel asked.

\*\*\*

From his hospital bed, JJ could see the sky and the clouds passing by. He had difficulties moving, his body still sore and cold, despite being tucked under blankets. He could still hear in his head someone speaking as he and Fred were lifted out of the water:… too many of them. The boat would be filled and so many dead people would scare the fish.' And indeed, he recalled a distant memory of himself lying on the deck of a boat; he had turned his head and saw several bodies floating in the water. JJ wished he had no ears to hear and no eyes to see; each time he tried to rest, the image of the lifeless bodies overwhelmed him. He and Fred had been saved, but so many were left out there.

When a nurse came in to check on him, JJ asked for Fred. She did not answer but brought in a doctor, a young doctor, whose white coat reminded him of the uniform of the sailors of the *Cambodge*. The doctor's loftiness contrasted with the friendliness of the sailors, and his unconcerned tone as he spoke caused JJ to loathe the white colour from then on, never forgetting the coldness of the doctor's words when he broke the news.

'Your friend did not make it. He was already dead when he arrived at the hospital.'

JJ tried to process what he had just heard when there was a knock on the door. Familiar eyes appeared, but they were not Fred's. He took a few seconds and finally recognised Marcel, his eyes red and full of tears. His friend's brother sat quietly on the bed, and they cried together, mourning their loss, as the doctor and nurse tiptoed out.

At some point, JJ noticed another silhouette had entered the room. Eyes still blurred with tears, JJ relied on his sense of smell and picked up a faint scent that reminded him of his mother. The fragrance grew stronger as he felt a hand stroking his head. He wiped his eyes and found his mother next to his hospital bed.

'Mamam.'

'I am here, my Jeanou. It will be all fine. The doctor said you can leave the hospital tomorrow. I will deal with the paperwork and will pick you up.'

Choked with tears, JJ could find no words.

Marcel got up to make space and left the room, looking as sad as he did when he had entered it.

His mother sat on the bed and kept stroking JJ's face.

'I heard there is a fine hotel near a beach called Repulse Bay. What if I booked a room there for us for a couple of weeks? Would you like that, mon Jeanou?'

JJ just nodded and slipped back to sleep, his mother's scent enveloping him and caressing his dreams.

\*\*\*


Sitting at a table on the roofed terrace overlooking the bay, JJ and his mother waited for their drinks.

'It reminds me so much of Phnom Penh. It is almost the same, except there is no war, isn't it, Jeanou?' his mother asked, looking at the ceiling fans that rotated lazily, dispersing the mild afternoon heat.

'I don't recall the hotels much. I was mostly at home,' he said, looking out to the sea.

'I know, that was horrible.' She sighed, unaware of JJ's body tensing. 'We did not experience war as bad as in Paris, but it has been such a difficult period for all.'

JJ frowned. 'I had the impression you had a good time.'

'A good time?' his mother said.

'I remember there were parties, and music, wine.' He gave her a sidelong glance. 'You also smoked opium there, didn't you?'

The waiter brought their drinks, interrupting JJ. The silence felt heavy as they picked up their cocktails with matching straws and paper umbrellas, and clinked in a toast.

JJ took a sip, now avoiding his mother's eyes.

'I think it is the first time that we spend a few days together, and the first time we have ever had a drink together,' his mother said.

He turned to her the moment she flashed a smile. He had often seen her use her charm with men, and he wondered why she was bothering with it now. He was wary of the whole set-up: the fancy hotel, the cocktails, her happiness to see him. He wondered if she needed anything from him.

'Jeanou, you were so young, and you did not see what was happening around you. And then, after George's death, you were so lonely and unhappy. I did not know how to help you and I just plunged into despair,' she said.

JJ looked at her, confused, unable to reconcile any feeling of desperation with his mother. But before he could comment, she went on.

'Indochina was not good for our family. Your father often left me alone.' She turned her glass in her hand, unsure how to go on. 'I suspected he had several affairs going on. To cope, I started drinking more, which made him angry as he thought this was not the right behaviour for his wife. And thus, he left me alone even more; his sister was on his side, and after little George's death, I was so overwhelmed by everything… your father, you… '

Baffled by what he was hearing, JJ stared at his glass and said, 'I know, I cannot blame you for not wanting me around.'

She uttered a soft sound of protest. 'I simply wanted to forget everything. It was not about you specifically.'

'I know George's death was my fault, and you were angry with me for causing that,' he said, looking right into her eyes this time.

His mother put her glass down on the table, spilling some of the green liquid inside, and took her son's arm in her hand. 'What are you saying? Of course, it was not your fault, Jeanou. Where did you get this idea from?' she asked, her eyes widening.

'I left him alone in the garden when you told me there were snakes. You looked at me so coldly that day and Father confined me to my room. You were so angry that I could not even go to George's funeral.'

His mother's eyes became bright with tears as she covered her mouth with her hands. She took a while to compose herself, but then she spoke calmly and assertively. 'Jeanou, I never, ever thought that. Yes, he was bitten by a snake, but it was not your fault. He also knew better than to go running through the brambles. George had a weak heart; this is why he died. The drug against the snake poison had caused his heart to fail.'

JJ looked at his mother, speechless.

'Did you think all this time that it was your fault?' his mother asked.

'The aunt said so, I remember she said I was selfish to have left him alone and your look then… '

'I don't remember my look, but I remember what your aunt said. She said that you were as selfish as I was. She was just picking on me. It was not about you.'

'But the maid, she left and the funeral… '

'We thought the funeral would be too hard for you. You were so upset. Your father let the maid go because he did not want you to play with her children; he used this story to fire her. I did not agree. We had a fight, but

246

the relationship with your father was so bad that I had no power against him. I was so overwhelmed, and my smoking opium became heavier, as well as my drinking. I felt guilty not being able to help you, or help myself.'

He felt her hand pressed against his arm, her pleading eyes focused on him as he rotated his neck and finally looked at her face. She pursed her lips.

'I thought you never cared,' he said, his voice barely audible.

'You are so wrong. I've always cared and always will. I was simply unprepared for so many things. You must forgive me, Jeanou.'

He shook his head and said, 'I still left George alone. Now my friend Fred, he died too. And my friend Du Bo,' he took his head in his hands, 'I seem to bring only unhappiness to those around me.'

To this his mother's hand slapped the table. 'Enough! I was messed up, I messed you up, but I am now older, and you are an adult. We make mistakes and we learn from them, but there is no point in telling ourselves that we bring others unhappiness or in feeling responsible for the world going wrong.'

Her firm voice rattled him, and he felt unsure how to take her tirade.

'Look at me, Jean Jacques. Look at me,' her eyes on him. I know where you get this belief from. It has been entrenched in me since I was young. But I now know that it does not serve me to believe that. People said I was a bad mother, maybe I was. I am here now, though, and I can teach you this: if your actions are only motivated by your need to be loved, you will always be at other people's mercy, or even hated by other people.'

JJ's breathing stopped for a few seconds while his brain let this sink in. His mother got up and gave him a soft kiss on his head before disappearing inside the hotel.

He was grateful for the time alone to think. He did not want to admit it, but he realised there was truth in what his mother had said. He could have made a different choice, instead of following Fred. He could have stayed with George, instead of following those kids. He could have taken a different path, if only he had felt a tiny bit of the love his mother had for him. What now?

Learn from our mistakes, she said.

\*\*\*

In his hotel room with a view of the sea, JJ took his diary, which he finally got back when his mother picked up his luggage at Marcel's hotel. The first thing JJ did was to check the urn. He cried with joy when he found it undamaged. His passport was also there, a thin piece of paper that had the power to decide the destiny of a person.

His mother had left that morning, wishing him good luck and telling him she hoped to see him home soon. After she departed, he sat at the desk and started writing with a new fountain pen his mother had bought him on one of their shopping trips. Instead of writing in his diary, though, he took out a postcard of the Kowloon Peninsula. The angle of the photograph was similar to the view JJ and Fred had from Victoria Peak that day, which now seemed so long ago.

*Dear Fred,*

*It looks like you were right. I can connect more with the dead than with the living, and you'll probably despise me for sending you this postcard. I will let you go, but I wanted to let you know that the time we spent on the Cambodge was one of the happiest in my life. Please, rest in peace.*

***

From his seat in the corner of the restaurant, JJ could see everyone who came in and out of the office building opposite. When he finally spotted Roger, JJ got up and crossed the street.

'Fred died,' JJ said, without a greeting.

'Hello, JJ. I heard. Hong Kong is like a small village and the news travels fast. I am so sorry for your friend.'

'Was it worth the money?' JJ asked.

'Don't ask me that. Rather, ask yourself: was it worth the risk to follow your friend? Was it worth keeping your promises?'

JJ contorted his face. Silent tears ran down his cheeks. 'I didn't keep any, none of them.'

'Then whatever happened, it was worth it, believe me. The most bitter lessons are those which teach us the most.' Roger paused for a second. 'It would have been better nobody got hurt, but to answer your question, yes. It was worth the money. You would think the same, if you had spent some time in a Japanese POW camp.'

JJ's eyes flickered for a moment, as he did not know about Roger's past. He nodded slowly, not knowing whether with his gesture he meant to agree with Roger.

'What are you up to now?' Roger asked.

'I wait for my visa to go to China again,' JJ said.

'To keep your promise?' Roger asked, lightly shaking his head, his eyes boring deep into JJ's.

'Yes.'

'Keeping promises is a double-edged sword, my friend. Always ask yourself what it's for,' Roger said.

'This time… I go to China for me.'

'Do you have the scroll?'

JJ shook his head. 'No, I lost it in the water.'

Roger nodded. 'If you need a place until you leave, you can stay with me. Water is not rationed anymore,' he added with a wink.

*** 

*Dear George,*

*This is the last time I will write to you. I am back in Hong Kong after messing up all I could mess up in my life. I have my passport back, and Old Min's ashes. But I have lost a friend, forever.*

The kettle whistled, and he got up to make coffee in Roger's kitchenette. He took his first sip, then resumed his writing.

*My mother was here, but she left after spending a couple of weeks with me. Yvette was right. We had both kept quiet all these years about how much we cared for each other. I had to almost drown to find out. For the first time I saw my mother as a person with her own life, her own pain and difficulties. It was not me, after all. What she did not love was her life, not me. I could not see that with my child's eye, and once I grew up, I had refused to see the reality around me. I had clung to that look she gave me after you died.*

*But she came here, and that surprised me. She peeled back the past, layer by layer, word by word, handing me the pieces of a puzzle that I did not know existed, and suddenly another picture appeared, one which did not correspond to the one in my head.*

*As my old wounds heal, new ones need my attention. But now I know I am not alone, and I realise that there are so many ways to tell a story. I don't have to choose the worst one.*

*I am now back at Roger's, maybe because he is the only other person I know in Hong Kong, or maybe because he is the only other person who knew Fred.*

*I won't stay here for long. I am going back to China to give Old Min's ashes to his daughter. I will also give some money that Roger gave me as a sort of compensation, funnily enough. But probably he parted with the money because now he has plenty.*

*I decided to attend the art academy in Hangzhou after all. Drawing and painting are what I do best, and focusing on that will help overcome the loss of another friend. I also need time to make sense of all the losses and of the newly found love around me.*

*Yvette promised she will come to see me and I am glad to have the chance to spend some more time with her.*

*My dear George, I think it is time to say goodbye. I will always remember your smile.*

JJ closed his diary and put it on the table. This would not be the last letter of his life, but the last one to a past he did not need to cling to anymore. Drinking his coffee, he smiled to himself as a warm feeling pervaded him. He felt more than sure that this was the right path for him.

# Acknowledgment

It might sound weird, but first of all I want to thank myself,. Without me, there would be no book at all, and no further persons to thank for it! Thanks to myself for all the times I sat up in front of the computer, even when I felt tired or had no inspiration. For the long hours I put in refining and editing the story, for the investments I was willing to make in order to give this book the best chances. For the learning I was willing to do and for the dreams I allowed myself to make.

But yes, I did not work completely alone. Thanks to my husband for listening to my ideas, making suggestions which sometimes sparked new ideas, for being my IT guy and for always giving me his support, whatever I chose to do. Oh, right… also for taking full charge of daily tasks and cooking in November 2019, when I entered the NaNoWriMo competition.

Many thanks to Eldes Tran for her editing, it was great to work together, and I am sure the book has really benefitted from her expertise.

Thanks to my writing teacher Jesse Falzoi, who encouraged me to publish my writing, and who by sharing her enthusiasm for short stories & co. in her creative writing courses, motivated me to pick up a writing practise.

Thanks to Martyn Beeny for his support in preparing a marketing plan, as well as Donna Cunningham of BeauxArts Design for her beautiful book cover.

Thanks to my very early readers who provided helpful feedback and some keywords for my metadata.

May I also thank our cleaning couple, Adam and Magdalena? Their work allowed me to have more time to write, so it has been a precious help!

I also want to thank those people who are behind a couple of the most interesting websites I used for my research, which I would like to share here:

www.gwulo.com

www.messageries-maritimes.org

www.saigon-vietnam.fr


And thanks to all my present and future readers, I hope my novel will allow you to travel with your mind and spend a few enjoyable hours and maybe got more curious about Hong Kong and China, two amazing places I definitively recommend visiting (even though there is a huge difference between 1954 and now).

# About the author

Lauca is a European writer, author of micro stories inspired by everyday life. Her historical thriller draws inspiration from her adventures across China, where she lived for six years, and her love for Chinese history. Her writing also reflects her interest in foreign languages and crossing cultures, thus it is not unusual to find characters of different nationalities in her writing. She also loves creating micro stories which sometimes stretch the reality.

She presently lives and works in the amazing European Union, where she feels at home even though she misses East Asia. Berlin is her city of choice, and when she is not busy in her daily job as an internal auditor, she works on her writing projects and as a qigong teacher.

# I would love to hear from you!

What did you like best about the book? What part resonated with you? Which character was most dear to you? You are welcome to drop a line through the contact form at www.lauca.eu or leave a message on my Facebook page at AuthorLauca or Instagram at Lauca_eu to let me know.

If you enjoyed this book, please also consider leaving a review to help other readers with similar reading taste discover the book.

Of course, a review will also support my writing and I highly appreciate you taking the time to write a review.

You can write your review on any other website you purchased the book from, on Goodreads, or you can send an e-mail to info@lauca.eu, I will publish your review on my book website page Returning East.

If you are interested to know more about China, subscribe to my newsletter to receive a short story about one of my adventures there. In addition, you will also receive an unpublished short story.

**Many thanks to you!**

Printed in Great Britain
by Amazon